FROM THE DEEPS

SEVEN WARDENS BOOK 1

SKYE MACKINNON

LAURA GREENWOOD

Peryton Press

Cover Design by Arizona Tape

Illustrations by Warlocklord

Published by Peryton Press

Formatting by Gina Wynn

From the Deeps is a work of fiction. Names, characters, places, and incidents are the products of the author's imagination or are used fictitiously. Any resemblance to actual persons, living or dead, businesses, companies, events, or locales is entirely coincidental.

CONTENTS

This book is also available as audiobook!

From the Deeps is a reverse harem, one woman and multiple love interests. Macey does not have to choose.

Please note that the authors of this book are from the UK, and as such, spellings and some turns of phrase will appear in British English.

You can find a glossary at the end of this book.

To everybody who loves waffles (and waffling) as much as we do.

Aunt Nessie would be furious if she could see her nephews fight like this. And so was Macey. Her brothers were idiots. Bruce had Jerry by the neck and was squeezing a lot tighter than he should have been. And what could she do about it? Not a damn thing. Not with the stupid bind that stopped her from using magic. It was the one condition that her father had given when she'd said she wanted to come on land. Well, that and the two buffoons she called brothers. Luckily, he'd bound them too, so at least they weren't about to start spurting water at each other. Or shift.

They wouldn't be able to stay in their kelpie forms for long without suffocating. She shivered, imagining the headlines that would come from the dead, oddly hued horses whose coats shimmered, not unlike when light hits the surface of the water. Oh, wait, that's exactly what it was like.

It was times like this Macey questioned her decision. But it was tradition for her people to come on land when they turned eighteen, and it'd been three years since then. Problem was, she really had no idea what she was actually supposed to do here. Some of the old legends talked of epic quests, and royalty, and men in kilts. So far, she'd seen none of that. Well, she'd seen a man in a kilt. But he had to have been around eighty, and she really didn't want to think about what was under it. Not. At. All.

Damn. Where was the whisky when she needed it? Oh right. It was behind her brothers. Not a reasonable solution then.

She cupped her face in her hands, not wanting to watch the fight anymore. The only result would be a bruise or two from their stupid game. It likely wouldn't even resolve what they were fighting over. Knowing them, it'd be something like the last of the stew she'd made for dinner. Maybe she should eat it herself... it wouldn't go down well, but might teach them a lesson.

Macey pushed back from the table and left the room; she had far better things to do. Maybe she'd curl up with her e-reader, which, unlike the man in the kilt, was something she actually liked about life away from the water. The book she'd been reading the night before was giving her ideas, probably ones that would cause her brothers to murder anyone that laid eyes on her, but she didn't mind.

She really needed to get herself her own place. Living with her brothers was hard enough below the surface, but, there, she was able to stop their shenanigans with her magic. She was more powerful than the both of them combined, and luckily, they knew that. Up here, their muscled bodies gave them the advantage. She was a measly five foot two in her human form, and while she'd been called pretty, she wasn't so sure about that herself. Guys would say anything to get women into their beds. And so far, she hadn't felt tempted by any of the local boys. They were too... Well, just not attractive to her. Too human. Not kelpie enough. She knew that was racist, but she was yet to meet a good looking human man her age. Brownie points if he was wearing a kilt.

Maybe she should move to a city rather than stay in this village. More people, more choice.

In her first year on land, she'd stayed close to the loch, feeling unsafe whenever she got too far away from the water. In her second year, she partied, hard. And now, in her third year since leaving, she was struggling to decide what to do. If she wanted to stay in the human world, she needed to get a job, or go to uni, or do something worthwhile. If she went back to her father, she'd have to behave like a princess again - something she hated. Caught between a rock and a wet place, that was her life. And caught between her brothers, if they didn't stop fighting.

"Oi!" she called out, but of course they didn't react, continuing their struggle. "Stop it, or I'll tell Auntie Nessie!"

The scuffle instantly ended, the mere hint of their Aunt's name enough. Macey snorted to herself. Of course it was. Aunt Nessie was terrifying, just ask the locals, but she had a heart of gold really, or at least she did for her niece, one of the perks of being the only girl, she guessed.

"You wouldn't." Bruce may have mumbled, but his voice was low and the walls were thin, so she heard it all. Damn, she really needed to leave. She sighed, ignoring him. He knew as well as she did that she wouldn't say anything. That would mean going back to the Loch, which Aunt Nessie never left unless she absolutely had to. Or she was terrorising the local fisherman. Macey sniggered to herself, remembering the last time Nessie had appeared to them. She'd used magic to grow three times her normal size and given one of the fishermen a shock so hard that he fell off his boat.

Macey retreated to her room and started to read. It was a book about humans, but it wasn't as boring as it sounded. She actually had to laugh a few times while reading. Who knew humans could be so amusing!

Suddenly, the lights went out. She waited a second for them to flicker back to life, but when nothing happened, she got up with a sigh to check if the other rooms were without power as well. The corridor was dark and so was the rest of the house.

"Bruce? Jerry?" she called, but there was no reply. "What's going on?"

She felt her way along the corridor until she reached where her brothers had been fighting not too long ago. She found the light switch, but when she pressed it, nothing happened. Maybe the fuse had blown, maybe her brothers were in the basement checking it out. That had to be it. They didn't usually leave without telling her first.

She made her way down into the basement, tripping several times over random things lying on the floor. She was really going to have to tell the boys to clean up after themselves. Just because they had servants underwater, it didn't mean they could behave the same way on land.

"Hello?" she called out again when she reached the bottom of the stairs. The basement always gave her the creeps. It was an old house and there was a distinct mouldy smell down there. Now, where was that fuse box again? She dimly remembered Jerry showing it to her after a power cut shortly after she moved in. It was probably hidden behind all those boxes...

Bingo! A dim green light signalled her salvation. Well, at least some light, which was a good start. She felt for the switches in the box, but they were all in the correct position. So it wasn't that after all.

Maybe the power had gone in the entire village?

Starting to feel anxiety creeping up on her, she stumbled back upstairs and opened the main door. "By the fucking waves," she muttered under her breath as she took in the view - or lack of - before her. A thick mist surrounded the house, making it impossible to see further than a foot or two. Her neighbour's house was on the other side of the road, but it could have just as well been on another planet. All she could see was white fog. She stretched out a hand and moved it through the mist, creating smokey swirls around her fingers. Did mist always behave like that? And did it always smell like aniseed?

She took a careful step forward into the mist. It was moving gently in the breeze, forming swirls and shapes - until she noticed there was no breeze. It was utterly windless, this wasn't normal.

"Jerry! Bruce!" she shouted, hating herself for the quiver in her voice. She was the Princess of the loch, she wasn't supposed to be afraid. But up here on land, she was no more than a mere human. With her magic blocked, she was defenceless.

She took another tentative step - and her foot hit something soft. She bent down, hands extended, until she felt something - someone. Falling on her knees, she shook Jerry's lifeless body, shouting at him to wake up. He was curled up as if he had been defending himself from something. Seeing her big brother taking on such a vulnerable position made her feel even more afraid.

She felt for his pulse. He was alive, thank the waves. Staying on all fours, she crept forwards until she found Bruce, lying in the same position. He didn't respond to her calls, nor to being hit (it was worth a try).

What was she to do now? Two unconscious brothers, a mysterious mist and an unknown threat. It sounded like a fairy tale, except that she knew most of them were true. And right now, she definitely didn't want this to be.

The fog around her began to shift, thickening into the shape of a man. He wasn't a person in the mist, he was *made* of mist. Before her eyes, the shape disappeared, leaving her decidedly uneasy.

An old story came to her mind of the fàth-fiata, an old legend her grandmother used to tell during the long nights of winter when the Loch's surface above them froze. It meant something like magic mist in Gaelic, her nan's native tongue. The story went that the Immortals used to create fogs to shroud themselves in, hiding from humans during their walks on Earth. Not that her grandmother ever actually explained who the Immortals were. Kelpies didn't believe in gods. There were stories in which humans were helped by mysterious beings, never knowing who they owed their good fortune to. But there were also tales of the fàth-fiata bringing great harm and evil. Right now, Macey preferred the first version.

But her unconscious brothers didn't seem to be a sign of a benevolent being coming to visit in the fog.

She needed to get them back into the house. She grabbed Bruce's shoulders and tried to drag him, but he wouldn't budge. Curse the genes that made her brothers into giants and Macey into a delicate dwarf. This wasn't going to work.

She closed her eyes, focusing on the magic locked inside her. She didn't even need to shift, all she needed was access to her powers and she would easily be able to get them back inside. But no, her father had put a lock on it that she wouldn't be able to break. As the King of Kelpies, he was the most powerful of them all.

She dug her heels into the ground, pulling on her brother's shirt, but all she managed to do was rip the fabric. She cursed, with language she'd never use at court. What was she to do?

Suddenly, something she couldn't see touched her cheek. She looked around, wild-eyed, but the fog and darkness hid anything that may have been out there. She went back to dragging her brother, but she hadn't managed to get him further than a few inches. There were whispers in the mist that made her cry out in frustration.

"Run," someone said close to her ear and she whirled around, jumping to her feet, ready to defend her brothers and herself. She wasn't one to run. She would fight.

With a crack, something hit her head from behind and she felt her legs crumble. She fell, landing on the limp body of her brother.

The last thing she saw were beautiful grey eyes filled with the swirls of the mist around them.

2

"How the hell would I know?" the male voice was low and rumbling, like the roaring flames of a fire. And just like flames, his words were terrifying, at least for Macey.

"You always know what to do," another man responded. His voice was softer, not as passionate, or maybe it was, just in a different way. It was hard to tell, her head hurt and she had no idea what had happened.

"You brought her here, Camdan, I thought you had a reason for that," the first voice replied.

"It felt right?"

"You *kidnapped* a woman because you thought it felt right? Are you out of your fucking mind?" The first man's voice grew louder and Macey wondered what the hell she'd managed to get herself into. Guess that was what she got for wishing her life was more interesting. She was away from her brothers for a start.

"We needed a fourth anyway."

"No, we needed water anyway," the first man responded, sounding a little condescending, but it was hard to tell without opening her eyes. For all she knew, the two men were sitting side by side, putting this all on for her.

"And she's water?" The man snorted. Actually snorted. She didn't think she'd heard anyone do that since she was a child at the palace. Bruce had received the scolding as a result of it. Apparently, it wasn't seemly for a Prince to act that way. If anyone asked Macey, she'd tell them it was antiquated and stupid. Unfortunately, no one ever actually asked her.

"She might be," the second man, Camdan, replied.

"I think I'd have recognised my opposite, don't you think? You knew when you met Jared, didn't you?" Silence stretched on after the first man's words, and an itch on Macey's thigh was making it impossible for her to stay still. Which was a shame, their conversation was more than a little intriguing and she wanted to know what they were on about. Probably not the most rational response to being kidnapped, sure, but it was the one her brain was apparently going with.

"Maybe not if..."

"Stop. She can't be water, that means..."

"That it's all true. Yes." Camdan said the words quietly.

"Believe what you will. I'm finding Jared." A shuffle and a slammed door after his words must have meant he'd left the room, leaving her alone with just Camdan, the man who'd taken her. That should have filled her with more dread than it did.

"I know you're awake," he said, and Macey gave up the pretence of sleeping, opening her eyes and finding herself staring into the same misty grey ones that she'd seen before blacking out.

"You," she croaked, her hand flying to her throat. Why was she struggling to speak? She really shouldn't be.

"Yes, me. Sorry about that, you were a little out of it." He chuckled.

"Out of what?" She pushed herself up so that she was sitting, allowing her to study the man more fully. Was he the same figure she'd seen approaching in the mists? That didn't seem right. He had the same grey eyes she'd seen, sure, but he was far more solid than the mist-man. Far, far more solid. In fact, he was verging on drool-worthy, with wide rugby player shoulders, and pale hair that was an odd colour between white and grey. Actually, it kind of matched his eyes.

"Consciousness? You fainted."

"I did? I don't faint." At least, she didn't think she did. She'd never done it before. "No, something hit me, I think."

"Sorry to break it to you, but you fainted."

"Fine," she huffed, crossing her arms over her chest, not quite convinced, but her memory was all fuzzy. Camdan's eyes flickered down briefly before returning to her face, and heat rose in her cheeks. That wasn't a reaction she was used to. Normally when men checked her out, it filled her with a slight sense of unease. "So, where am I?"

"A safe place."

Well, that was informative of him. "Who are you?" she tried a different question, hoping he'd be more forthcoming on this subject. Though if he knew she'd been awake the entire time, then he should know she was already aware of his name.

"Camdan," he answered anyway.

"Camdan," she tested the name out. "Anything else?"

"No, just Camdan. Some people call me Cam though." He shrugged, as if it was of little importance.

"Who are you, Cam?"

"Just a man," he replied. Damn, he was an infuriating one. "Ignore Flint, his temper runs a bit hot." He chuckled to himself.

"Going to let me in on the joke?" she asked, growing more irate by the second.

"Not yet, no," he replied.

"Well, then I'd quite like to leave," she said, getting up from the bed she was lying on and shooting Cam a challenging look. She was not going to show how insecure she felt.

"I'm afraid that's impossible."

She huffed, anger bubbling up in her. "And why is that? Am I your prisoner?"

"Not at all. But if you look outside, you'll see we're no longer on Earth."

"What the fucking waves? Is that a joke?" In two steps, she was by the window, ripping open the curtains. A wall of mist blocked the view. This house could be anywhere. She looked around the room. It was simple, generic, boring. A small bed, a wardrobe, a chair - currently occupied by Camdan - and a sink. Nothing special. And definitely not something that was going to tell her anything about where the heck she was.

"I wish it was," Cam said sadly. "I'm sorry I took you, I don't know what came over me."

She whirled around. If only looks could kill.

"So why did you kidnap me? What did you do to my brothers?"

He looked at her, his forehead scrunched in

confusion. "Your brothers? I didn't do anything to your brothers. Didn't even know you had any."

"But they were lying on the ground... Unconscious..." Her voice faltered as she realised what that meant. If he was telling the truth, Cam wasn't the only one who'd been out in the mist.

"I didn't see anyone. I saw you collapsing so I caught you and brought you here," he explained, looking down on the ground, evading her eyes.

"You still haven't explained why you did that," she snapped, her voice harsher than she had intended.

"Did you hear me talking to Flint?" he asked and she nodded. "It felt like the right thing to do. I was travelling on the *Staran*, the hidden path, and felt a weird kind of tug, so I left the path and found myself in your village. I planned to hide in the mists but the fàth-fiata were already there. Then I heard shouts and found you. End of story."

"That doesn't explain anything," Macey huffed. "What's the *Staran*? Why were you going to hide?"

"Sorry, I'm not used to talking to humans," he apologised but stopped when she growled.

"I'm not human," she said through clenched teeth. "Don't insult me."

He held up his hands. "Sorry, I didn't know. You were in a human village, so I assumed... What are you?"

"Wouldn't you like to know." She shook her head. "Answer my questions first."

"Sorry - I seem to be saying that a lot today." He grimaced. "The Staran are the paths between worlds, a quick way to travel through the mists. I think humans call them ley lines, but that's a simplistic term. They're not set routes, they change all the time, and sometimes, they bring you where you need to be, not where you want to be. Like today, I guess."

"What the actual fuck? You expect me to believe that?" her voice rose higher at the end as her outrage seeped in. He'd brought her here, without checking if it was okay first, and now he was expecting her to believe he'd travelled along these Staran to some place that didn't seem to really exist. Next, he'd be telling her that the gods existed and actually controlled stuff, and she knew that was a lie.

"Look out of the window, it's a little hard to deny then."

"Not true, it could just be really crap weather."

Camdan started laughing. "I know you're from Scotland, but you have to admit that this would still be a little extreme for *just* bad weather." Damn, he had a point.

"How do you know I'm Scottish?" she demanded instead, going as far as stomping her foot on the ground. Maybe not as mature as she should be, especially with the weird pull she was feeling towards

Camdan. At the same time, he couldn't exactly say anything about it, not after kidnapping her.

"Your accent is a bit of a giveaway." He gave her a self-satisfied smirk and her hand flew to cover her mouth. She hadn't even realised that she *had* an accent. "Do you have a name?"

"No, my Mum decided she wanted to be different and gave me a number instead," she snapped and he stood there in stunned silence, confusion written over his face for a moment.

"Which number?" he asked once he'd regained his composure.

"What?"

"Which number did your Mum give you?" He smiled at the end, his soft grey eyes boring into her and distracting her from her train of thought.

"Two," she replied dryly. When he stared at her, she sighed. "She called me Macey."

"So why did you say Two?" he asked her in confusion.

"Ever heard of sarcasm?"

"It's a very human concept," he said slowly and she shook her head in frustration.

"One last time, I'm not human."

"You certainly behave like one."

"Well, I'm not. And anyway, what are you?"

He smirked. "You're not telling me your species, so why should I tell you mine?"

"Point taken," she sighed. "But you really need to let me go. I need to find my brothers, I need to make sure they're okay."

"Not possible." He crossed his arms in front of his chest, showing off his hard muscles. She swallowed at the sight. It was hard to focus on being angry with him when looking at those distracting muscles.

"Why not?" She was getting really impatient now. Couldn't he just answer her questions with more than a word or two?

He shrugged. "The Staran won't let me leave."

She huffed. "Well, I never said that you needed to leave. I can go on my own."

"Only my kind can use the Staran. You need one of us with you to travel on the paths of mist."

"But what about the other guy? Flint?" She knew she was clutching at straws now. She needed to get out of here, away from these crazy men who had kidnapped her for no apparent reason.

"He can try, but I doubt it will work. The Staran have brought us here, together, and they have a mind of their own. We haven't done what they want us to do, and until we fulfil our purpose, they won't let you leave."

She shook her head, swallowing a growl. "But that's just a theory, right? You're just making this up, you want to keep me here. Pervert."

He chuckled. "Seriously? You're calling me a

pervert? Don't think I haven't noticed you checking me out."

She blushed, very aware of the truth in his words. But then, she didn't really have a choice. He shouldn't be allowed to look that good. Hot. Sexy. Fuckable.

Macey cleared her throat, trying to get her stream of thought back to the issue at hand. "I'll try it anyway, when Flint is back. Will that be soon?"

"I don't know," Cam said, looking at the clock above the door. "He was a little annoyed when he left, which usually means that he'll stop by the tavern on the way to pick up Jared."

She frowned. "Why does he need to pick up Jared? And who is he, anyway?"

"Jared is not like Flint and me. He's not... he can't travel on the Staran on his own. Just like you."

She sighed, sitting back down on the bed in defeat. "Can you contact Jared somehow? I really need to know if my brothers are well."

Camdan frowned and sat down next to her, cautiously putting an arm around her shoulders. She was tempted to shake him off, but somehow, it felt good. Calming.

"I've already asked him to, but he hasn't replied."

"Huh? How did you ask him? You've been with me ever since he left and you've not used a phone."

He smiled and tapped a finger to his forehead. "We don't need human toys to talk to each other.."

"Ohhhhhh. That's what we do, but only underwater."

"Underwater? You're a mermaid? A selkie?"

She shuddered at the insult and instinctively grabbed his throat, letting her nails grow as a statement. "Never call me a selkie if you want to live."

Instead of being afraid, he looked at her in fascination. "Interesting," he murmured. "A kelpie." He stared at her hair until she followed his glance and sighed in frustration. It had turned green. Again. She really needed to work on her self-control.

"And not just any kelpie. A member of the Royal family," Cam mused. "Well, that certainly makes things more interesting."

She released his throat, shrinking her nails back to human size. It was a little painful, and quite a waste of time, seeing as he hadn't even flinched. Usually, people reacted differently.

"So, one of your brothers is the crown prince?" he asked and she nodded in resignation.

"Both. They're twins, and it was a caesarean, so they were both born at the same time. It's created a bit of a constitutional crisis, and my father still hasn't declared one of them his heir."

"Which means someone would be very interested in them," Cam said, more to himself than to her. "But they weren't taken, they were left unconscious. You went outside to find them... leaving the protection of the house... an easy target. Maybe you didn't faint after all..."

"Just when you had convinced me of the opposite," she complained. "Something hit me before I fell, before I saw you."

"We should thank the Staran for bringing me there just at the right moment."

She nodded. Whatever these strange sentient paths were, she had to be grateful to it. That didn't mean she couldn't be angry at it at the same time. She needed to get to her brothers. Which brought her back to Flint.

"Is there a way you can force Flint to look for my siblings?"

Cam laughed, a deep, beautiful sound. "Force Flint? Oh sweetheart, nobody can force Flint to do anything. People who do that get burned."

She sighed, hating herself for being so weak. She wasn't used to feeling powerless. She was so good at finding solutions to problems, usually. Not now, though.

"Then what are we going to do until he returns?"

"How about we get some food?" he asked and she smiled.

"Finally you're talking sense."

3

She watched as Camdan pottered around the kitchen, making sandwiches bigger than any she'd ever seen in her life. Not that she was complaining; damn, she was hungry. Then again, partially shifting outside of water was energy consuming, hence why she didn't do it often. Even if it was the only magic she could perform at the moment. Which reminded her...

"How did you know I'm royalty?"

Camdan whistled a tune, making her unsure about whether he'd heard her, but she waited patiently. He'd answer her whether he wanted to or not. She hated thinking that her heritage was so obvious. It wasn't like she'd been acting like a Princess since she'd gotten here or anything. "Cam," she said more firmly.

"Huh?" he grunted, finally turning his attention back to her.

"How did you know I'm royalty?" she repeated.

"Oh. Your eyes."

"What?" She blinked rapidly, unsure how to take that. She'd never once considered her eyes could give her away. They were blue, a pretty blue, sure, but that was all that was special about them. Well, other than that they clashed awfully with her hair when she was in halfling form, but she had no control over that.

"Your eyes glowed when you shifted," he said, setting down a plate, with an overflowing sandwich on it down in front of her. Macey's mouth watered at the sight of it. She really was hungry.

"No they don't," she insisted before taking a large bite of the sandwich and caught herself almost moaning at the taste. It was as delicious as it looked. Making Cam a hot guy, who could make food. Other than the kidnapping, he was a great catch.

"Have you ever watched yourself shift, Two?" he asked, chuckling slightly at his joke.

"Of course." It was one of the first things she'd ever done after learning about the halfway shift. It wasn't something all kelpies could do, only the most powerful ones.

"And you've seriously never noticed your eyes glowing bright blue?" He raised a pale eyebrow as he took a bite of his own sandwich. His eyes closed, and she was glad it wasn't just her that was affected by good food.

"Yes, I *seriously* never noticed, because they don't do that. And even if they did, that wouldn't automatically make me a Princess." She tried to be mad, but how could she be when he was so delicious? No, wait, when the food was so delicious. Damn, she needed to get her head in check, she couldn't let herself be so distracted by him. It'd only get worse once Flint returned, she was sure. Just his voice alone had her tied up in knots, and she had no idea what he looked like yet. She could hope he was ugly as sin, but somehow she doubted that.

"Maybe not, but the fact you haven't once denied that you *are* royal does kind of give it away, Macey." The way he said her name sent a shiver down her spine.

"Oh."

"I'd suggest you eat up before Flint gets back too, or he'll steal the food right off your plate." He smiled at her, the act lighting up his face and making him look younger than he had before. Not that she had any idea how old he was. If he wasn't human, and she fully believed he wasn't, then he could be anything from twenty-five to three thousand and sixty-two, though she doubted it was the latter.

"You still haven't told me what you are?" she said, taking another bite out of her sandwich. She wasn't going to ignore his warning. He clearly knew Flint well, and if he said Flint would steal her food, then she believed him.

"No, I haven't."

"Are you going to tell me?" For his sake, the answer had better be yes. Cam sighed, setting down his food and running a hand through his pale hair, leaving it mussed in a way that had Macey wishing she'd been the one messing it up.

"I can't really. But mostly because I don't really know myself. I'm some kind of wraith I think."

"Like a ghost?" She frowned, he hadn't felt like a ghost. Nor did he look like one. Which was a highly illogical thought given she'd never actually seen a ghost. For all she knew, they were as solid as she was. Cam laughed goodnaturedly.

"I can assure you, I've never died. But I've also never met anyone quite like me. Well, and Flint."

"I've met no one quite like me either," she countered, not liking the idea of not being special.

"I doubt there's anyone like you, but I mean power wise, I've never met anyone like me, whereas I suspect you've been around kelpies your entire life," he said softly.

"True," she admitted. Actually, this was the first time she'd ever been away from her people for so long. It felt, odd, but freeing. And while she wanted to know that her brothers were alright, she wasn't ready for that freedom to end. "Has Flint replied yet?" she asked hopefully.

"Sorry, he hasn't. But the two of them should be back any moment." He nodded towards her plate as if to encourage her to eat up. She didn't need telling again, and quickly polished off her food, allowing Cam to clear their plates away.

"Tea, coffee, wine?" he asked as he placed the last of the plates in a dishwasher. It seemed a little odd that they had a dishwasher when they appeared to be living completely away from civilisation, but she figured that was something it was best not to question him about. At least, not if she didn't want to end up with an insane headache and still no answers.

"Just tea, please," she answered. She'd had her fill of wine during her party years. Now it was good quality whisky or nothing, like the good little Scot she was.

He turned to put the kettle on, but was interrupted by a loud crash from the hallway outside. "There goes any peace," he muttered.

Two men stumbled into the room, the broad auburn-haired man clearly supporting the other one. The sober man was clearly Flint. She didn't know how she knew that, she just recognised it as true. Which meant the not so sober man was Jared. She studied him as he stumbled. He was as tall as Flint was, but with a shaved head and dark skin that seemed to have taken on an unhealthy pallor. Due to the alcohol, no doubt.

He looked up and fixed her with an intense dark brown stare that seemed completely at odds with the rest of his intoxicated appearance. "Who the fuck are you?"

"Mind your manners," she hissed. "Maybe sober up before you speak to me like that."

He seemed taken aback for a moment, then laughed heartily, bringing some colour back into his pallid skin. "I'm not drunk, little one." He wavered as he took a step forward, and only Flint's strong grip prevented him from falling.

"No? You look pretty drunk to me," she teased, but stopped when he lifted his head and she saw a tiny trickle of blood spill from his mouth. If he wasn't drunk, then that meant... "What happened to you?"

Ignoring her, Cam stepped forward and helped his friend sit on one of the comfy chairs around the kitchen table. "How long have you been like this?" he asked, face grim.

"About two days?" Jared groaned and wiped away the blood from his chin.

"Fuck, did you learn nothing from last time? You need to feed!" Cam growled angrily, but there was a trace of desperation in his harsh voice.

"Feed?" Macey asked hesitantly, and Jared looked at her with sad, bloodshot eyes.

"I'm a baobhan sìth, lass," he sighed, as if that would explain everything.

"What's a baa-van shee?", Macey asked and he sighed again.

"Don't they teach you anything nowadays?" Flint interrupted while putting a wet cloth around Jared's neck. "He's an incubus, one of the only ones in existence. And right now, he's starving himself. Again. For some fucking noble reason he won't explain!" His voice had turned loud and bitter.

"It's better this way," Jared whispered hoarsely. He seemed to be getting weaker with every minute that passed.

"What does he need?" Macey asked, fearing she already knew the answer. She'd read about incubi, but never thought that they existed here in Scotland. But then, she'd grown up beneath the water's surface, far away from all the beings roaming the lands. Hell, she'd only ever learned about humans, and even then meeting them had been a shock. They were so... boring. But this baa...something, was certainly not boring, not at all. He was hot, sexy, beautiful. His skin invited her to touch, and his mouth to kiss, deeply, passionately. She approached him, hips swinging in a silent dance. Her hands wandered to her blouse, slowly unbuttoning it while keeping her eyes fixed on him, her prize. She was going to make him feel good. She was going to make him better. She kneeled down in front of him, putting her hands on his knees, spreading his legs to give her better access - SLAP. A hand landed on her right cheek and she yelped.

"Snap out of it!" someone called, but she didn't care. She put a hand between his legs, feeling the bulge making itself known. He was getting ready for her. She smiled as she reached for his zipper - and screeched as she was pulled back, someone's arms around her chest. Wait, her chest. Boobs. Her nipples hardened at the touch and she turned around, facing her captor. Cam's stormy grey eyes were fixed on her, so beautiful, so pretty. She stretched until she was on tiptoe, and pressed her lips against his. He didn't respond so she nibbled on his bottom lip, just a little, to make him open his mouth, and he did, but only to say, "Stop it, you will regret this later."

She didn't care, she wanted to kiss him, and more, to fuck him, hard. Someone ripped her away from him and she moaned, needing his touch.

"Get her into the guest room," Cam shouted, and she was picked up, her arms pressed to her side. She growled in frustration, her nails sharpening into claws. She was going to get her pleasure, even if she had to fight for it. She struggled against the iron grip, pouring some of her kelpie strength into her muscles. She didn't have to fully shift to have the strength of a shifted kelpie. Why hadn't she that used earlier when she was trying to drag her brothers? Stupid! But it didn't matter just now. With a roar, she broke his grip and turned around, pouncing on the man who had stopped her from getting her kiss - and saw Flint, staring at her in surprise. She liked that look on him. Delicious. Totally fuckable.

She jumped and wrapped herself around his hips, burying her claws into his back. She ignored his scream and slowly licked his cheek where a scratch was just starting to bleed. How had he got injured? She didn't know, but she was going to kiss it better. She swirled her tongue over his wound, tasting the blood, savouring it.

Suddenly, he was gone and she fell to the ground, her ass crashing onto the hard wooden floor. She screamed and looked around, searching for Flint - but he had disappeared into thin air. Only Cam and Jared were with her in the kitchen, both watching her in a mixture of fascination and horror. In her haze, she noticed that Jared was no longer looking as sick, but then her hormones took over and she jumped to her feet, slowly stalking towards them. She was going to have them both, at the same time. She licked her lips as she imagined being sandwiched between the two men, their bodies rubbing against her own. She smiled at them seductively, but they didn't smile back.

"I'm sorry, lass," Jared whispered and for a moment, she was confused, but then she saw Cam's arousal and continued to walk towards him. She remembered she was going to unbutton her blouse, but when she lifted her hands to her collar, something was pressed against her face from behind, something soft and smelly. She caught a whiff of it, a familiar scent... thyme?

"Breathe in deeply," Flint said from behind her, "it will make everything better."

She followed his command, sucking in air through the fabric, filling her lungs with the smell of thyme. She coughed and Flint released her from his grip, that she hadn't even noticed. Something in her mind changed. Everything was becoming clearer. She took a deep breath and looked around the room.

Then it hit her.

Mortified.

Embarrassed.

Wanting to sink into the ground and die.

"Take me away from here," she whispered, hating how weak she sounded. But with the scent of thyme still filling her nose, and the pounding in her head that must have been the result of Jared's magic, she didn't really have much choice.

"Okay," Flint whispered back, scooping her into his arms and carrying her from the room. Without fully realising what she was doing, she wrapped her arms around his neck, burying her head in his shoulder. He was a lot warmer than she expected, like there was something bubbling beneath the surface that was raising his temperature, an raising hers in turn. If she wasn't careful, she'd end up taking her clothes off for an entirely different reason.

He set her down on a soft bed. She stretched out, hating the feel of her clothes against her sensitive skin. Jared's pheromones may have worn off thanks to the thyme, but she was still feeling the effects of it. She wanted to feel the cool air against her skin, and she really needed to find some relief, though maybe that was best left until she was completely alone.

Flint took a step back from the bed, and Macey let out a soft whimper, taking herself aback. She'd never been the needy type, even as a child she'd been infuriatingly independent, not wanting anyone to control her. It had driven her father and brothers crazy, especially when she'd insisted on going on land and their father had made them go with her.

"I'm coming back, Macey." His voice rumbled through her. She nodded, cursing herself for being so needy, even if she knew it wasn't completely her fault. He left, giving her a lingering look as he walked through the door. Oh, she was in trouble if he kept this up, especially if Jared was going to keep making her go crazy. Though maybe she could persuade the three of them to be a little less reluctant going forward. A girl could dream.

She shuffled up the bed so that she was propped

against the wall, that way she could keep an eye on the door and anticipate Flint's return. He was back within moments, a wadded up shirt in one of his hands. "Here," he said softly, handing it to her. "I thought you'd be more comfortable with this."

"Thank you," she said, unfurling the fabric to discover that it was a man's t-shirt. From the size, she suspected it was Flint's, but she had no way of knowing for sure. She stood up shakily and began to unbutton her blouse, anxious to be more comfortable.

"Whoa, Macey, hold up." Flint held up his hands as if to tell her to stop, but she didn't understand why. She cocked her head to the side.

"Why?"

"I can see you," he pointed out needlessly.

"I should hope so, unless you've suddenly gone blind."

He snorted slightly and she smiled. He was a lot calmer than he'd been when she arrived, and she found she liked this side of him. "I can assure you, I've definitely not gone blind." His voice went straight through her, reawakening the side of her that Jared had brought to the surface. But this was different. Very different. She could tell the difference now between the forced attraction of before, and the burning need inside her. Weirdly enough, this felt far more intense.

"Good to know," she said huskily, continuing to remove her blouse. He licked his lips, but didn't do anything to stop watching. She hoped he didn't. Dropping the blouse to the floor, she unzipped her jeans and pushed them down over her hips, wiggling her way out of them and hating how unsexy removing them was. Surely the people who'd created jeans should have considered that important factor when they came up with them? Luckily, Flint didn't seem to mind, at least not if the intense look he was giving her was anything to go by. His eyes were dark, though it almost seemed like there were flames flickering within them. Though that couldn't be right and she knew it. Cam had said he and Flint were the same, and there'd been no hint of fire from him.

Stood in front of him in nothing but her underwear, she should have felt self-conscious, and yet that hadn't even crossed her mind. How could it when there was someone looking at her like that? It was like a shot of caffeine teamed with an injection of confidence, and it was making her blood sing. Other things too, and from the look on Flint's face, she wasn't the only one that felt that way.

Something snapped between them and he strode forward, pulling her to him with a burning hand on her bare skin. He leaned down and crushed his lips to hers. This wasn't tentative or unsure, this was primal. She could feel how much he wanted her, and not just because of the bulge that was pressed against her. He was conveying so many emotions and desires in the one action, that even she was surprised.

Macey pushed her body against his, dropping the t-shirt he'd given her to the floor so that she could grab handfuls of his own, pulling him as close as possible. Damn, how she wished she could get it off him without breaking the kiss. It'd be a shame to end such bliss. A fleeting thought passed through her mind and she focused on her hand for a second, shifting it so her nails sharpened. Having no choice, at least none in case she wanted to accidentally maim him, she watched what she was doing as she ripped a nail down the material, ripping it from his body, before threading her non-shifted hand into his hair and pulling his lips back to hers. His hands left her body, but only for the amount of time it took for him to shed himself of his ruined shirt. The moment it was gone, he placed his hands on her waist and pressed himself against her again.

Even through the kiss, she could hear how ragged his breathing was, and that it matched her own. She'd never felt like this before. Not with any of the humans who'd tried to kiss her during her party years, and not when she was with her childhood sweetheart under the water. Nor was it like the drugged up kisses she'd experienced while under Jared's influence.

Whatever it was, Macey wasn't ready for it to stop.

She rubbed against his bare chest, their skin touching, sending shivers through her body. Their tongues danced as her fingers roamed his back, slowly making their way down to his bum. Fighting against his tight belt, she squeezed her hands into his jeans, gripping his firm ass, pulling him closer.

With a gasp, he leant back, leaving her breathless. "What's wrong?" she whispered as he gently took her wrists and pulled them out of his trousers.

"I'm not going to take advantage of you like this," he said, gently stroking her hair as disappointment crashed into her.

"But you're not," she moaned, stretching up to kiss him again, but he evaded her.

"I am," he whispered, "you just don't know it yet. There are things I have to explain to you... but not now. You need to rest, little kelpie." He winked. "If you still want me after we talk tomorrow, I'll be ready."

Before she could reply, he left the room, leaving her speechless and shivering in humiliation. Was she truly this unappealing that not just one, but three men had rejected her within the course of an hour? Granted, she was glad they had ignored her advances while she was under the influence of Jared's pheromones. It made her trust them more. Not every man would reject the advances of a young woman ready to jump him.

Sighing, she picked up Flint's shirt and put it on. It smelled like him. She debated whether to take it off, but that would have been childish. And it was comfy. And his.

She curled up on the bed and pulled the duvet on top of her, hiding from the world. This day had been too much. Fear, surprise, anger, desire, disappointment, humiliation. Her body was shivering from all the emotions her mind was remembering. She growled and pressed her hands hard against her ears, listening to the pulsating whoosh of her blood. It reminded her of the waves, of home. She imagined being back underwater, an innocent, slightly spoiled kelpie princess, who didn't have to deal with abductions, desires and hot guys.

Just like the waves in her thoughts, sleep washed over her, taking her with it.

4

When she entered the living room, still wearing nothing but Flint's t-shirt and her underwear, the three men were waiting for her.

Camdan cleared his throat and pointedly looked down at the floor. "Why are you walking around naked?"

She shrugged. "I don't have any clothes."

Flint chuckled. "Girls. I'll get you some later. Weren't you wearing jeans yesterday?"

Now it was her turn to look at the carpet, hiding her blushing cheeks. "I ripped them by accident. My claws must have come out without me noticing."

"Yes, Flint told us what happened between you two," Cam sighed and she swallowed hard. She was tempted to run back to her room and hide from all the embarrassment. Forever. Instead, she looked up, giving them all dirty looks.

"Do you always gossip like pesky little selkies?" she hissed, ignoring the fact that her hair was turning green in anger.

"We don't gossip," Flint grumbled. "They needed to know."

"Did they now," she growled, but inside she was getting curious. He'd promised her she'd find out more about them today. Maybe she should stop being angry?

"Sit down, Macey," Cam commanded. She hissed at him but did as he said. That didn't mean that she had to stop glaring at them, though.

"How do I start...," Flint murmured, more to himself than her.

"Easy," Jared grinned, "you're fire, she's water, opposites attract each other."

Cam groaned, hitting his friend in the ribs. "Do you ever think before you speak?"

"Rarely."

"I've noticed. Now be quiet and let Flint explain it properly."

Jared smirked but didn't reply. Macey was staring at them open-mouthed. What the fuck was going on here?

Flint sighed again, obviously feeling uncomfortable. "What do you know about the Seven Elements?"

"Aren't there just four?" she asked, taken aback by this strange question.

"That's the human way of thinking. In truth, there are seven: fire, air, earth, water, ice, wind and lightning. We call them *Seachd-Sìona* in Gaelic."

"Wait, aren't air and wind the same?" she interrupted? "And water and ice?"

"Similar, but not the same," Flint explained. "Their base essence is different. Which is why there are seven of us."

He paused to let it sink in, but she was having none of it. "Seven what? Idiots?"

Cam chuckled. "Seven Wardens."

"Please tell me you've heard of the legend?" Jared groaned dramatically. Macey shook her head, embarrassed at her lack of knowledge of the supernatural world. Her grandmother had told her stories, but most were about the peoples roaming the sea and waters, not... Wardens, whatever they were.

"May I remind you that you didn't know it either when you joined us?" Cam reminded him sternly and Jared grimaced.

"That's different. I didn't grow up in your world."

"Have you asked Macey how she grew up?"

Jared shrugged before admitting, "No, I haven't."

"Then don't be so quick to judge." Cam turned to Flint. "Brother, would you do us the honour?"

Flint smiled and got up, bowing dramatically.

Macey smiled. This was going to be interesting.

Clearing his throat, Flint began to chant in a deep, smooth voice.

> *"Fire and wind,*
> *brothers in arms,*
> *lost in the mist.*
> *Earth will join,*
> *Always hungry,*
> *Only sated by meeting the fourth.*
> *Water will run, circling Fire,*
> *then Wind and Earth.*
> *Lightning is trapped,*
> *Ice will break the chains.*
> *Finally, Air is waiting,*
> *only to appear*
> *when the end is near."*

Silence followed his recital, broken only by the flickering of the flame he suddenly conjured, hovering above his outstretched hand.

"I am fire."

Cam got up and lazily moved his fingers through the air, creating a tiny tornado in the palm of his hand.

"I am wind."

Jared stood up as well, opened his mouth - and laughed, bending over as his chuckles grew louder. "Sorry, but you're a little too dramatic," he wheezed in between laughs. "And I can't show her earth without destroying the house."

"You just destroyed my performance," Flint complained, but a grin was slowly appearing on his face, making his eyes sparkle in the light of the fire he was still holding.

"Sorry," Jared shrugged, still laughing. "Oh and by the way, you're water, Macey.

"I got that, believe it or not," she muttered. Maybe that wasn't the comment she should have been addressing, after all, they had just told her she was a Warden, whatever one of those was.

"Just making sure," Jared said, a boyish grin spreading across his face. She liked it, it lit up his eyes and made him seem ten times less intimidating than when he'd arrived the night before desperate for a feed. He looked far healthier now, which didn't make any sense. How was that possible? Had he gone back out to find another woman? She hoped not, that idea wasn't sitting very well within her; in fact, if he'd done that, there'd soon be a woman out there with claw marks on her face and the fear of gods that didn't exist in her. If she'd had her magic, maybe she'd even try her hand at one of the curses Aunt Nessie had taught her.

"You don't look as bad as you did yesterday," she prompted, hoping he'd get the hint and she didn't have to ask more outright. Jared chuckled, giving her a knowing look.

"Something you did seemed to work on me."

"I didn't do anything," she said with a frown. This time, it wasn't just Jared that laughed.

"You did plenty, Two," Cam said and she scowled at him. He'd have done plenty too if he'd given into her. It wasn't *her* fault that they'd all turned her down, even if she was secretly glad about that.

"Has that ever happened before?" she asked Jared, completely ignoring Cam's comment.

"No, this is the first." He looked far too pleased with himself for her liking.

"Right, okay, moving on," she said. She crossed her legs, being careful to make sure the t-shirt slipped further up her legs. Three pairs of eyes bored into her, and she smiled to herself, satisfied with their response. She'd have them caving to her in no time. Which was definitely a good thing. She didn't feel quite as horny as she had yesterday, but there was still something simmering under the surface, and that was an itch she definitely wanted scratching. Three times, preferably. "So where are the other four?" She looked at Flint, figuring he was the most likely to answer. He'd taken the lead before after all.

"You mean three," he said gently. "With you, there are already four of us."

"Oh."

"But we don't know. We always needed you before the next part could come to pass," he added.

"Me?" she squeaked. "As in, me, Macey?"

"No, as in you, water. That you're you, Macey, is just a bonus." His eyes trailed over the length of her body, lingering on her exposed thighs. Score one for Macey. She'd have fist pumped the air if she didn't think they'd take the piss out of her for it. Maybe she'd save it for when they left her alone. Unless they never did. Hmm, not a bad thought.

"So there are three more elementals out there, and you have no idea where or who they are?"

"That sounds about right," Jared said, looking way too pleased with himself. She shot him a dirty look. If he wasn't careful, she'd let him get too desperate again before she fed him. That'd serve him right, though would probably punish the rest of them in the process. Okay, maybe not her best ever idea.

She ran through the prophecy Flint had recited in her head a couple of times, already surprised that it was so imprinted in her mind. "Guess that means we'll find Lightning next?" she asked tentatively, glancing up at Flint, who nodded proudly.

"I suspect Lightning will come with Ice, but in effect, yes."

"And that's not going to complicate things?" she glanced around the three of them, instantly regretting what she'd said. Except, no, she was a Princess, she wouldn't be ashamed of what she was saying, or thinking, as the case may be.

"Complicate what exactly?" Cam asked, a mischievous sparkle in his eyes.

"Nothing," she muttered. "So what's the end?"

"We have no idea," Jared answered this time, looking serious for once. Or at least, for once while he wasn't starved out of his mind.

"It's always been a little bit of a mystery," Flint added. "But you're here now, so we were hoping it'd all become clear."

"Just like that?" She couldn't stop the laugh that escaped as she asked. It all seemed a little far-fetched really. She wasn't the answer to anything, except who was the kelpie with no powers. Ah, her powers. This was probably the time to tell them she had none. Well, that she had no access to them.

"We don't know," Cam answered, his storm grey eyes watching her intently. "We weren't exactly expecting this."

"Me neither."

"Any more questions?" Jared asked. "I'm starved, and it's Cam's turn to cook." Oh good, she could get on board with that, especially if the food was as good as the sandwich he'd made her the night before.

"Do any of you know anything about unlocking water powers?" she asked quietly.

"Think this one's yours, Flint," Jared said, standing and slapping his friend on the back.

"Good luck," Cam added as he stood and moved towards the door, dragging Jared along behind him.

"What's all that about?" she asked once they'd left, hopefully to go to the kitchen, she really could do with some food.

"I think they're trying to avoid the fire versus water thing."

"Oh, will it be bad?" She hadn't actually considered that part yet.

"I don't think so, if opposites attract, then it doesn't make sense for it to be explosive. At least, not in that way." Even though he didn't do it, she could hear the wink in his voice and let out a small giggle. "Your powers are locked then?"

"Yes, my Father locked them before I came on land."

"Why?" His eyebrows drew inwards in a perplexed expression that only brought her giggles back. Damn, when had she become such a girl?

"I don't actually know," she responded once they'd subsided slightly. "It was one of the conditions of me coming onto land. I suspect it was so I'd go back home quicker, but it's hard to tell with him." It had always bothered her that there was no explanation to the block on her powers; it didn't seem to achieve anything really. Except for her not being able to do certain things.

"But you shifted, last night when we—"

"I know," she interrupted. "That's a different type of kelpie magic. I can shift, but not fully unless I'm underwater, but I can't do any of my other magic."

"Can I see it?"

"No, I can't do magic on land."

"You shifted, I meant," he replied.

"Oh, no, you don't want to see that. It's not exactly an elegant form." She shuddered at the thought. Kelpies weren't exactly the most attractive of things to shift into, and she didn't think she was ready for Flint's opinion of her to change quite so drastically.

"One day I want to see it," he said, his voice holding a sultry promise that she wouldn't be able to ignore.

"So what do we do now?" she asked, changing the topic. After all this talk about shifting, she suddenly had the picture of him riding on her kelpie form in her head... she'd rather have him ride her in a different way. In their current forms. Right now, preferably.

She shook off those thoughts, cursing herself for

being so desperate for being touched. It had to be a side effect from Jared's feeding, it had to be. She wasn't usually this flirty.

"Now we see if my fire can coax out your water," he whispered, pulling her close. His eyes were burning coals, warming her in all the right places. She was craving his touch, wanting his lips on hers, wrapped around each other, not letting go.

"I'm not sure my father intended me to unlock my magic like this," she chuckled, and he grinned.

"Like what?" Flint teased, hovering only a breath away.

"Are you going to kiss me?" she whispered, posing a rather rhetorical question.

"I shouldn't..." He gave her a tiny kiss on the nose. "But I want to."

Then he crashed his lips on hers and she forgot all about her magic. This was magic, the sensation of him claiming her mouth, of their bodies pressed together, of being united by a fierce, all-consuming kiss.

All too soon he pulled away, leaving them both breathless. "We should get to work before the others come back," he sighed.

"Isn't this how you're going to help me?"

He frowned for a second, then laughed. "No, this was just because I like to kiss you. Your lips are so soft, so... kissable."

"Is that all you can come up with?" She winked and he chuckled again.

"I'm not a man of many words. I'm a man of actions." He suddenly conjured a large flame in his right hand and she flinched, stepping back. "Don't worry, I won't burn you."

"Until three years ago, I'd never seen fire before. We don't have flames underwater."

He huffed. "How do you keep warm? Where do you get your light from?"

"We're kelpies, we're warm when we're shifted. And even in my human form I don't get cold easily. Especially not in water. And for light, we have bioluminescent plants and fish. I used to have a light-up squid as a pet."

"Didn't you grow up in a Scottish loch? I didn't think they had squid in there."

She smiled. "He was a present from a distant relative. And besides, most people don't know kelpies live in the lakes around them, so how would they know about a few squid."

"Point taken. Is it okay for you to come closer to the flame?"

Not wanting to be seen as weak, she approached him, eyeing the fire warily. When she first came to the surface, her brothers had played a prank on her, pretending the lit candle on their table was there to be touched. She couldn't remember why she believed them, but she could still feel the pain echoing in her hand. Those bastards, why was she trying to rescue them again? If they needed rescuing - she still wasn't any closer to finding out.

Macey stared into the flame, somehow feeling a pull inside of her, urging her to come closer.

She lifted her hand, passing it closer to the flame than she probably should, but it was so tempting and the urge to touch was too difficult to ignore. She waved her hand over the top of it, feeling the prickle of heat on her palm, along with Flint's intense gaze.

"Oh," she said as she watched the flames turn blue slightly.

"That was unexpected," Flint said softly and she turned to look at him, her eyes locking with his and revealing a combination of curiosity and desire. Good. She was glad he was still feeling it, or the fire simmering in her blood was misplaced. She gave a short laugh. The fire in her blood? How ridiculous was that when she was a water being. Kelpies didn't want or need fire, there was no reason for her to be feeling it. Well, no reason other than the tall, handsome man who was looking at her like he could devour her.

"What do I do now?" she asked, definitely feeling uneasy about the whole situation.

"Do it again, but move closer this time."

She frowned. That wasn't what she expected him

to say, nor was it something that particularly appealed. But then again, she didn't think he'd let any harm become her. Which was another odd thought. She'd been kidnapped and separated from her brothers, and yet here she was thinking about how attractive one of her captors was? Not only that, but how much she trusted him. Macey shrugged it off, remembering a piece of wisdom her Aunt Nessie had told her once; *"Always trust your gut."* Of course, being Aunt Nessie, that hadn't been all there was to her lesson, it had come laden with stories of her own misspent youth, but the point had been driven home. Sometimes, Macey had to trust her own instincts, even if they seemed wrong.

Which meant moving her hand closer to the flame. Taking a deep breath, she did just that, almost touching the top of it this time, and once again, the flames themselves turned blue. But nothing else happened. She didn't feel the surge she normally did when her magic was close to the surface, making her sure that it hadn't come.

"Closer?" she asked before she could stop herself.

"I guess so," Flint said, a worried note in his voice. She studied the flame, which was almost entirely blue now, but the intensity of it didn't seem to have waned, and she felt the heat of it against her skin still. She took another breath, knowing she just had to get on with it, or she'd chicken out. Before she could put too much thought into it, she thrust her hand into the middle of the flame.

It was hot, but it didn't burn, which was completely at odds with what she'd discovered after her brothers played their prank on her. Looking back at Flint, she could see the worry on his face as he glanced between her and the flame, seemingly confused about what was happening. Well, that made two of them.

"What did you expect to happen?" she asked carefully, dreading the answer.

"I wasn't sure..." he hedged, making anger boil up in her.

"You thought it was going to burn me, right? Why would you do that?" Her voice turned into a shout. "I trusted you!"

The door was thrown open and Cam barged in, looking around for the cause of the noise. "Is everything okay?" he asked, his relief obvious at there being no immediate danger.

"He burned me!" Macey hissed and pointed at Flint.

"What the fuck?" Cam growled and strode towards his friend who held up his hands, the flame still flickering dangerously from between his fingers.

"Calm down, she wasn't hurt," Flint defended himself, but he did do her the courtesy of looking a little downtrodden. "She's fine. But I thought if her body assumed it was under attack by the opposite element, her magic might spring into action."

"So you burned her to test a theory?" A breeze began to roam around the room, making Macey's hair flutter in the wind. Cam was getting angry, and so was the air around him.

"Look at her hands, she's fine!" Flint shouted over the wind that was getting louder. "Macey, show him your hands, he needs to see if you want the house to stay intact!"

With a sigh, she showed Cam her unmarked skin. This was for the benefit of structural integrity. But she wasn't going to let Flint get away with it. He had broken her trust and he was going to pay for it.

The wind died down almost as quickly as it had arrived. Cam took her hands into his, examining them closely. When had he become so protective?

"How are you not burnt?" he asked under his breath, more a statement than a question. It was clear that none of them knew.

"Does that mean that Jared's magic can hurt you? Even though he's your opposite?"

Cam laughed grimly. "Oh yes, he can definitely hurt me. We weren't always friends. When we found him, he was... broken. He drank too much, and when he did, he got violent. Strangely enough, it was after our biggest fight that he finally began to trust us."

"But maybe that's because we're not sure if he

actually is your opposite," Flint mused. "With fire and water, it's clear. Earth's opposite could be wind, but it could also be air, or lightning. So maybe we haven't met your match yet."

"Why are you assuming there are pairs anyway?" Macey asked. "If there are seven elements, it doesn't work out."

"It's something Malan said according to the legend, just before he foretold the Prophecy of the Wardens. That he knew that six pairs were going to come, led by one who was different. In the prophecy, Air is mentioned as joining on its own, last, so we assume that it's the leader who will tell us what to do."

"Ehm, who's Malan?" she asked, once again annoyed at her own ignorance.

"A prophet who lived a long time ago. Maybe two hundred years? Or has it been longer?" Cam replied, deep in thought.

"It was just after we met. Three centuries, perhaps?" Flint said, and Macey gasped. Then giggled. Then gasped again.

"Did you just say that you met three hundred years ago? How bloody old are you?"

Cam shrugged. "Not sure. It never really mattered in the Mists. Only when we left and started exploring other worlds did we notice how fast time passes for other beings."

"So I'm just a quick blink in the passage of time?" she asked, the words sounding less bitter than she'd expected, and just coming across a little sad. They'd already affected her a lot, and this was the most excitement she'd had in, well, ever. But if all she was to them was the fleeting moment of yet another year, then really, what was the point for her? She shouldn't let herself fall too deeply, or she'd just end up hurt, and they'd be the ones laughing all the way to the ends of the earth without her.

"Hardly, weren't you listening to the prophecy?" She glared at Flint, not appreciating the way he was talking to her. He'd better stop or he'd soon find himself in a wet heap on the floor.

"Yes I was listening, but unlike you, I haven't had centuries to get used to the idea," she snapped. She spun around, almost losing her balance until normal temperature hands caught her, resettling herself on her feet.

"Whoa, Macey, calm down." Cam pulled her closer. Reluctantly, she went with it.

"Calm down?" she shouted. "Calm down?! You've taken me from my home, kept me here, told me some stupid prophecy that has no real explanation, burned me, then revealed that I'm nothing but a nanosecond in the immense span that is your lives. And now you expect me to be calm?"

"I didn't burn you," Flint said from behind her,

sounding much like a spoiled child. She ignored him, it was that or end up ripping his head off with her bare claws.

"Erm, Macey?"

"What?" she snapped at Cam, no longer able to contain her anger even if she knew that she should. After all, it wasn't *Cam's* fault she'd nearly been burned.

"Your hair's turning green."

"Eurgh." She took a few deep breaths, trying to regain control of her shift. That was twice in as many days; accidental shifting had never happened so often. Maybe she needed to do a full one? Get some of the pent up energy out of her system, that way, she wouldn't keep doing it by accident. "Do you have a swimming pool?"

"What?" Flint responded before Cam did. Though Cam's confused face reflected Flint's tone.

"A swimming pool. You know, big, filled with water, you can swim in it?" She turned around, not moving away from Cam's arms, and his hands trailed over her in a tantalising way she almost couldn't ignore.

"I know what one is, just not why you want one." She raised an eyebrow, wondering how long it'd take him to catch on. "Oh." Understanding dawned on his face.

"So, do you have one?" she repeated, just about

refraining from tapping her foot with impatience. He really was trying his very best to wind her up.

"Yes, we have a swimming pool," he answered eventually.

"Great, where is it?"

"Down the hall, I'll take you in a second," Cam whispered in her ear, and she nodded.

"Can I watch?" Flint said hopefully, referring back to his desire to watch her shift.

"No."

"Why not?" he demanded, his voice firm and more than a little inviting if she was honest. A part of her wanted to take him up on the promise there, but the rest of her squashed it down, reminding her that she was still mad at him.

"Because I'm not shifting in front of anyone," she responded. Maybe one day, she'd feel comfortable shifting in front of them. But the last thing she wanted was for the men she was so attracted to to see her in her rather ungainly form. Kelpies weren't the most elegant of species.

"But—"

"No," she said firmly, and to her surprise, Flint nodded, finally accepting her decision.

"Come with me." Cam linked his hand with one of hers and pulled her down the corridor that headed in the opposite direction to where the bedroom she'd stayed in was. How big was this place? And how hadn't she noticed how big it was before? It was like a labyrinth. Which just made her wonder what else was hidden about here.

She followed him without saying a word until he directed her into a room smelling strongly of chemicals. She wrinkled her nose, already hating it, but knowing she needed the water to shift. Technically, being underwater might unlock her powers again too. She didn't actually know, this would be the first time she'd shifted since leaving the loch.

5

Cam led her into a wood-panelled changing room which looked a bit like a sauna. There were towels and a variety of slippers in different sizes on a shelf by the door. She chose a pair that looked like it would fit and grabbed a surprisingly fluffy towel. Noticing that Cam hadn't left yet, she turned, giving him a pointed look.

"I'd like some privacy now, please."

He chuckled. "Sure I can't change your mind? I've never seen a kelpie before."

"And you never will," she muttered, before shooing him out of the room. Reluctantly, he left and she locked the door behind him. Finally, she was alone.

The water was warm, far too warm for her taste; she was used to the icy loch waters. But it would do.

Usually, she preferred to wade into the lake until she was half submerged, then shift, but this swimming pool was deep all over, there was no gentle slope. She'd have to shift while swimming, something she didn't enjoy at all. Shifting was a complicated process and having to focus on staying afloat made it even more difficult. Her kelpie form could breathe underwater, but her human did not.

She quickly undressed and climbed into the pool, savouring the sensation of water on her naked skin. By the waves, she had missed this feeling. It made her feel complete, like a missing part of her had slotted back into place. She swam a few rounds, enjoying how she was so much faster than on land. She may look human, but her kelpie spirit gave her an affinity with water that was far beyond that of human swimmers. When all her muscles felt like they'd been stretched properly, she swam to the centre of the pool, not wanting to hurt herself on the hard edge wall.

She took a few deep breaths, preparing herself for the shift. The memories of her very first, very painful shift never quite went away. Kelpies stayed in their aquine form until puberty before being able to change shapes. She remembered how she had suddenly struggled to breathe, how her father had raced her to the surface where she had thrashed and howled from the pain of her bones reshaping and her scales retracting. It no longer hurt as bad, but it still wasn't something she enjoyed. But right now, her body needed it.

Over time, she had learned to control her shift precisely. She started with her feet, forcing her toes to merge, her nails to grow into hooves. Next came her hands, adding webs between her fingers, then her arms, her legs, until she had four horse-shaped limbs. Except for the webbing, of course. The rest was easier as it required less precision. Expand her torso, grow a tail, lengthen her spine, change the shape of her head. Easy, except for the fact that her lungs were beginning to ache for oxygen as she sank deeper and deeper into the pool. The chlorine taste distracted her from forming her gills properly. Ignoring the burning pain in her chest, she concentrated hard, preparing her gills to breathe for the first time. It needed to be right, or she'd get water into her still-human lungs.

Finally, she was ready. She took a short, careful breath, and when only when she'd confirmed the gills worked, she breathed in deep, filling her lungs with much-needed oxygen. She whinnied in delight as she began to dive, using her thick tail as a rudder and the flipper-like flaps on her legs to propel her forwards. This was her element, this was her very own paradise.

She stayed underwater until the chlorine began to dry out her skin. That was the problem with chemicals, they had a tendency of damaging her scales; it was true whenever a ship spilt petrol in the loch too. There she could just swim further away and deeper, but here, she didn't have that option. Instead, she had to shift back into human form and get out of the water. She was already dreading the shift back.

She breached the surface of the pool, glad she could breathe above water in her Kelpie form, albeit for a short space of time. But that short space was enough for her to shift her head and lungs back into her human form, her long green mane shortening and turning darker, resting on her shoulders, the next thing she shifted back to normal. Huh, normal? When had she started to see her human form as the normal one? That was an odd thought, to say the least.

Macey winced as the pain ripped through her, hating that her people hadn't evolved a less intense way of changing forms. It didn't really make sense for it to be that way, especially when they'd been able to shift since the dawn of time itself.

"Well that was really something," a deep voice came from across the room, making Macey squeak and jump back, splashing chlorine filled water into her eyes and causing them to sting. Damn, this pool really had it out for her.

Rubbing her eyes, she saw Jared's dark form leaning against a wall, studying her intently. "I told you not to watch," she half-growled, conscious that she was naked, and made even more so by Jared's dark gaze.

"Technically, you never told me not to watch," he replied, not moving from the wall.

"It was implied," she muttered, crossing her arms, which didn't quite have the effect that she wanted it to. Instead of making her look angry, it pushed up her boobs, and she wasn't the only one that noticed. At least, not if Jared's lingering glance down was anything to go by.

"You should never rely on implied, Macey, that's a good way to end up being watched."

"And the locked door didn't tip you off," she hissed at him, treading her legs in the water to keep herself afloat. If she focused, she could have forced a partial shift, but most of her attention was on the man watching her, and she didn't want to give him any more information about her kind that he already had. It hardly seemed fair when she knew no more about what he was.

"It did, but you said you wanted to know about your brothers." He studied his nails while smirking to himself. He clearly knew what he was teasing her with.

"I do, yes."

"I got a message."

"And?" she prompted, keeping as much control on

her anger as possible. It wasn't easy though, and she needed to get out of the water before she managed to instigate a full body shift rather than just a partial one like normally happened when she was angry. She swam over to the side of the pool and hoisted herself out of the water, infusing her arms with as much kelpie strength as possible.

Macey rose to her feet and let the water rivulets run down her naked skin, enjoying the sensation of Jared's eyes on her. She wanted to remind him to answer her question, but she was enjoying the look on his face far too much for that.

"What?" he said, the word catching in his throat and he coughed to clear it.

"What about my brothers?" She lowered her own voice, infusing as much sultriness as possible into it. Which was probably completely wasted on an incubus, but it was far too late for that.

"Oh, yes, brothers." He was visibly frazzled, and satisfaction purred in Macey's chest. He was putty in her hands, and considering his status when it came to sex, that was kind of impressive. "They're safe."

"Safe?" she demanded. "All you're going to give me is safe?" Anger rose in her, along with the faint surge of water magic as it began to rise along with it. Good, shifting had done something towards unlocking her powers. Ignoring it for the moment, she looked into

Jared's eyes, then frowned. His expression was uneasy to say the least.

"You do not want to see an angry kelpie," she warned him, knowing that her hair had changed colour again. This should have been an obvious warning, but Jared seemed to be transfixed by her nakedness. She should probably have been flattered - and maybe she was, a tiny bit - but right now, she wanted to know about her brothers. "Tell me or suffer the consequences."

"Dramatic much?" he teased, but he still had a slightly uncomfortable look to him. He sighed. "Flint left to do some inquiries. Then he contacted Cam, who told me. Not much more to it."

She frowned. "How did he find out so soon? He can't have been gone longer than an hour?"

Jared shrugged. "Three hours, actually, You were swimming for a long time. But also, time passes differently here. If he's on Earth, he might have been there for a day already. Enough time to find out about your brothers, apparently."

"Wait..." She did a quick calculation in her head. "If three hours are a day... And I've been here for at least twenty-four hours... That means over a week has passed since Cam kidnapped me!"

"Macey, your eyes are glowing," he warned, taking a step back.

She roared in frustration and, using her kelpie

strength, threw him into the pool. He landed with a splash and went under. She grinned as he came back up, spluttering and thrashing in the water. Schaden-freude was such an ugly word.

"I... can't... swim..." he gasped in between gulps of air and her gloating smile disappeared. Seriously? Were there people who couldn't swim? Guess she had just met one.

With a sigh, she dived into the water; luckily she wasn't wearing any clothes that could get wet. With two strokes, she was by his side, grabbing him under his arms to hold him up. She partly shifted her legs, making it easier to keep them both afloat.

"Why the fuck can't you swim?" she asked while treading water. He spat out a mouthful of water, narrowly avoiding her. Then he began to laugh.

"Of course I can swim. But would I have got you into the pool with me if I hadn't pretended not to?"

He stopped his fake struggle and she released her grip on him, annoyance taking over. He had played her. That bastard was going to pay. She dived and grabbed his legs, pulling him below the surface. It was kind of ironic that she was doing what kelpies were known for - even though that was just an evil rumour the selkies had invented. Kelpies didn't kill humans, why would they? Most of the water dwellers were vegetarians; human flesh didn't appeal to them. But right now, Macey had an appetite for incubus flesh. Maybe not in *that* way, though...

Jared's clothes were hugging his body tightly, revealing his muscles and his... manly parts. She stopped pulling him through the water to take a closer look. Who could blame a girl for wanting to learn more about another species...

That's when he began to struggle and she noticed that he may not be able to hold his breath as long as she could. Oh well. She released him and he swam back up to the surface. This time, his gulps for breath were real, not fake like earlier. Served him right, deceiving her like that.

When she resurfaced next to him, he grinned at her despite his breathlessness. "Like what you saw down there?"

She blushed and hoped that the water would hide her embarrassment. How did he notice her checking him out?

"You were going to tell me about my brothers," she quickly changed the topic. His grin disappeared.

"Let's get dry and go back to Cam. He'll be able to tell you more." He huffed. "I was just the messenger. Why do people always attack the messenger?"

6

She tied her hair back in a messy bun as she walked back into the living room they'd been in earlier. It was still soaked through from her time in the pool, and the resulting shower she'd had to rid herself of the awful chemical stench.

Jared reclined on the sofa, looking comfortable despite his equally damp hair, and his white t-shirt sticking to him where he hadn't dried himself properly. Macey licked her lips, her mind already back on how close she'd been to him in the swimming pool.

"Oh good, you're here," Cam said, pulling her attention and thoughts away from Jared and to where the other man was pacing frantically. She squashed the urge to run over to him and rest a comforting hand on his arm. Doing that would probably lead to her becoming even more distracted.

"Yes, Jared said you had news of my brothers." Maybe she should have started with something a little...softer, but she was desperate for news.

"Yes." He shared an uneasy look with the other man and Macey's heart sank.

"You told me they were safe?!" She meant to shout, instead, it came out more like she was a strangled cat struggling to keep a hold of her emotions.

"They are," Jared said and she glanced his way. The expression on his face did nothing to allay the dread that'd settled in the pit of her stomach.

"Why do I sense there's a but?" she whispered, not able to make her voice sound any stronger. Damn, she was pathetic.

"Because you're not going to like what Flint found out." Cam closed the gap between them and wrapped his arms around her. Despite knowing she probably shouldn't, Macey leaned into him, inhaling his scent and relaxing ever so slightly.

"But they're safe? And alive?" Possibilities flew through her head, ranging from the improbable to the absurd. But then again, if she existed, and the men surrounding her, then was anything really impossible?

"Yes, both. But Macey..." He looked away from her as if he was hiding something, though she guessed he was. If her arms hadn't been twined around his waist, pulling him as close as possible, then she'd be biting her nails in nervousness.

"It was them," Jared blurted out, receiving a sharp glare from Cam. Macey pulled away, standing between the two men.

"Them, what?"

"Them that caused all this," Cam said softly.

"All what?" She wouldn't believe it. It wasn't possible. It couldn't be, could it? Macey shook her head.

"They're the ones that sent the *fàth-fiata* after you," Jared said, placing a comforting hand on her arm, but she knocked it away.

"No, no, no, no." She shook her head violently, the whole world going a little fuzzy. They had to be lying. And yet the serious looks on the two men's faces was enough to tell her they weren't.

Which was when it all went black.

SHE BLINKED her eyes furiously as she came back around. It took her a few moments to get her thoughts in order. Mostly due to how comfortable she was on whatever the men had rested her on. She sat up, fixing them with stern glances. They still had a lot of explaining to do.

"So, let me get this straight. You think my

brothers pretended to be unconscious, created some weird fog and then planned... what exactly? World domination?" She laughed bitterly.

The guys wanted her to rest, blabbering something about her fainting twice in as many days, but by now she was sure that she hadn't fainted that first time. Someone had hit her. And because her brothers were lying on the ground, it hadn't been them. Problem was, the two men didn't believe that theory. They found it much easier to believe her brothers were the culprits. Not that it made sense, not in the slightest.

"They're already the crown princes and heirs to the throne, I'm just the third in line. So it's not that. And I thought the *fàth-fiata* was just the magic mists someone uses to hide in? Not a conscious being by itself?"

They were staring at her, apparently waiting to see if she had finished. No, she hadn't yet.

"So this... mist hit me on the back of my head, but then let you kidnap me, Cam? Without interfering? This doesn't make any sense! Am I the only one who can see that?!"

"No," Jared mumbled, "you make sense. Maybe we were a little rash in thinking it was them."

Macey crossed her arms in front of her chest, the effect slightly marred by the fact that she was in bed, propped up by pillows. The guys hadn't allowed her to get up... yet. She was going to need to pee in a moment, so she was sure they would let her do that.

"Where is Flint? He's the one who said it was my brothers. Who's his source?"

They looked at each other uncomfortably.

"He's not been back in touch since he told me it was them," Cam admitted. "I've been trying to reach him ever since you collapsed—"

"Fainted," Macey corrected.

"... fainted. He seems to have shielded his mind, which he usually only does when he goes drinking or... ehm..."

Jared made a suggestive hand gesture and Macey laughed, despite trying not to. But her laugh was followed by a wave of jealousy taking hold in her heart. To distract herself from that unfamiliar feeling, she asked, "Why don't you guys have phones? Who doesn't have a phone nowadays?"

"We're not on Earth. There are no mobile phone networks out here," Cam explained and Macey cringed. She could have come up with that herself. But then, they still hadn't explained where exactly they were and why they were living here in isolation in the first place.

"So what do we do now?" she asked, resulting in vague shrugs by the guys.

She groaned in frustration. "Okay, Cam, you keep trying to reach Flint. It's strange that he would tell you something important like that and then just ignore you after. Jared, make us some food. We're going to leave this place to search for answers, but not on an empty stomach."

"Did she just tell us what to do?" Cam stage-whispered, staring at her wide-eyed.

"I think she did," Jared whispered back. "I think I like it."

Macey sighed and got out of the bed. Halfway across the room, her head exploded in pain. She vaguely felt how her body crumpled to the floor, but she was fixed on the source of the pain, a thick, black hand gripping her mind as if it was a physical object. She struggled against its hold, but it only resulted in more pain.

"DON'T STRUGGLE, LITTLE KELPIE," a loud voice boomed, making her shiver at its cruel, cold tone. "YOU CANNOT ESCAPE ME."

"Who are you?" she shouted in her mind, her voice wavering from pain. "Let me go!"

A laugh reverberated all around her.

"THIS IS JUST THE BEGINNING. YOU ARE MINE NOW. YOUR MIND IS MINE, AND YOUR BODY WILL SOON FOLLOW. REJOICE, FOR YOU HAVE FOUND YOUR MASTER."

Despite her fear, she laughed. "Are you for real? People don't speak like that." It was taking all she had to pretend that she was unaffected by his words. The pain was making it hard to focus, but she pushed it away as hard as she could.

"I ALREADY HAVE ONE OF THE SEVEN. YOU ARE THE SECOND. THE OTHERS WILL SOON FOLLOW."

"Give him back," she growled, unsure why she knew it was Flint he was talking about, nor why she was so accepting of that. But Flint didn't belong to the Voice. Flint belonged to her. Instead of responding properly, the Voice just laughed hollowly through her mind, causing shooting pains through her head on top of the duller one that'd appeared when the Voice had.

"Macey!" Jared's voice cut through the pain as the laughter faded, along with some of the pain. "Macey, say something, please." She was surprised by how worried he sounded. After all, he wasn't aware of that she'd decided he was hers, surely he shouldn't feel anything more than a very mild concern over someone who he claimed to be protecting. If that's what she was going to refer to kidnapping as now.

"Here." It was Cam this time, and something damp pressed against her head.

"Maybe we should take her back to the pool?"

Jared asked. As her mind regained control a little, she noticed that she was lying on the floor, and her head was on someone's lap. Jared's she imagined. His hand was stroking back her hair soothingly. She was sure it was him, but didn't want to open her eyes to find out.

"No, not pool," she murmured. Shifting would probably get rid of the pain in her head, but only because the pain in her body would distract her. Which made it stranger still that the Voice had managed to cause so much pain. Her threshold was pretty high. It had to be when she went through shifts like those, and yet the voice had her almost collapsing. Or completely so, if her other two fainting spells were anything to go by.

"Will the shift not help?" Cam asked softly, sounding closer this time, though she wasn't sure if that was because he'd sat down next to her, or that her head was just clearing more.

"Chemicals," she got out, sounding fragile even to herself and hating that they'd be able to hear that in her voice. Weakness wasn't something she liked showing. It never had been, not growing up with her brothers. Which reminded her...no. She refused to accept any of that. Bruce and Jerry wouldn't betray her, she refused to accept that. Though she also suspected that it wasn't quite as cut and dry as she thought. Things never were.

"Oh shit," Jared muttered. "Why didn't we think of that?"

"Because we didn't expect to have a kelpie come to stay?" Cam replied. He rested a hand on her arm, and she appreciated the contact. She appreciated the contact with both of them actually. It was soothing in a way she would never have suspected before.

"Kidnapped," she muttered, still unable to form proper sentences. Damn, the Voice and the pain had taken a lot out of her. More than she'd admit to if any of them actually asked. To her surprise, Cam laughed, actually sounding amused.

"Yes, okay. I didn't expect to kidnap a kelpie." He waited a moment, and though she couldn't see him, she knew he was hesitating. "But aren't you glad I did?" he whispered softly, as if he didn't really want to say the words. Probably because it'd been less than twenty-four hours. She should say no. She shouldn't feel so comfortable with them. It shouldn't feel so right. And she certainly shouldn't let them know that their mere presence was doing more to make her feel better than anything else in her life.

"Yes," the word slipped out without her meaning it to.

"Good, now let me go drain the pool." A shuffling noise came as he made to get to his feet. With surprising deftness, Macey flung her arm out and closed one of her hands around his wrist.

"No. Don't go." Damn, when had she got so needy? She really shouldn't let them see this side of her, she had no idea what it'd actually do. Inwardly, she sighed with relief as he sunk down next to her again.

"What happened, Macey?" Jared asked, still stroking her hair gently. She attempted to shake her head, but that only made the dull ache intensify.

"Not sure." Slowly, she opened her eyes, cringing at what felt like a bright light.

"Try and explain?" he prompted.

"Where did Flint really go?" Because she was as sure that simply to find her brothers was as much baloney as the sailors who thought manatees were mermaids. If they thought the peaceful manatees were anything like actual mermaids, then they'd be in for a shock when they met the real thing. The mer were a rather...aggressive...race to say the least. Or they were if Aunt Nessie's stories were to be believed. She claimed to have met some mer while on her own quest out of the loch.

"To Earth," Jared said.

"Specific," she replied, turning her gaze on Cam. She reckoned he'd be the one who cracked easier.

"He went to see if your brothers were safe," he replied softly, though she still thought he was hiding something. She didn't say a word, her eyes locked with Cam's and she could see him about to give in to her. "He went to see if he could find more about the *fàth-fiata*."

"Wait, you don't know about them?" she blurted out, sitting up quickly before clutching her head in her hand, the ache becoming more intense in some places. Whoever the Voice was, they'd done a real number on her.

"Just the legends." Cam shrugged.

"But, you were talking as if you knew more..."

"I already knew they existed, but I've never encountered one before."

"So you could have kidnapped me to save me from something that may not have done any harm anyway?" Unlike the last few times, she felt her eyes flare and assumed that meant they were glowing. From the smirk on Jared's face, she was right. Good to know her eyes glowed when she was angry. At least they'd never make the mistake of thinking she wouldn't.

"Well yes, but—"

"No buts. Don't kidnap people when there isn't a good reason." She poked a finger into his chest, and he captured her hand in one of his.

"I promise I won't kidnap you again without good reason," he said with a cheeky smile, his swirling grey eyes boring into hers and proving to her how sincere he was being.

"Good. Now the *fàth-fiata*..."

"Are going to be a very big problem," a deep voice came from the doorway, and Macey turned her head to see what she couldn't quite believe. Stood in the doorway, looking a little worse for wear, but very much there, was Flint. But if he was here, then who did the voice have?

7

"Why is she on the floor?" Flint asked, by her side in a flash.

"Tell me the prophecy again," I asked weakly, ignoring his question. "What happens after us four?"

Cam frowned but recited it nonetheless.

> *"Lightning is trapped,*
> *Ice will break the chains.*
> *Finally, Air is waiting—"*

"He's got Lightning. It must be. He doesn't have you, you're safe. I'm so glad you're safe. Please stay, don't go away again," she mumbled, noticing too late that her filter had apparently switched off.

"You broke her!" Flint growled at the other two accusingly. "What the fuck did you do to her?"

"Nothing, she fainted, then she left the bed, then screamed and collapsed."

Flint growled again. "I wouldn't call that nothing. She looks like she's half-dead and her eyes are flickering. Why aren't you two more concerned?"

"You weren't here, you didn't see it," Jared replied, raising his voice. "She looked like she was having a fit, she was thrashing, mumbling weird things. It was scary, alright? We're concerned, we're very concerned! I was fucking frightened, hell, I'm still—"

She groaned as his loud voice was making her head pound in pain. "Silence," she whispered and they all shut up. "He's got Lightning. We need to find him. Or her."

"What are you talking about?" Cam asked gently. "Who's got Lightning?"

"The Voice. He was talking to me. He... touched my mind. He hurt me." Macey shuddered, and suddenly she had three pairs of hands holding her tight as the memory of his darkness threatened to overwhelm her. Now that the pain had receded, she realised how much of a violation this had been. How he had entered her mind, attacking her. And she hadn't been able to fight him off. A whimper escaped her.

"Shhhh..." Cam whispered soothingly, stroking her hair. "Don't think about it. Tell us what you know about Lightning."

"He said he's got one of us. I thought it was Flint, but you're here now." Macey squeezed his hand and he smiled reassuringly. "If the prophecy is true, Lightning is trapped. It makes sense that it's the Voice who's got him. And... he said that it'll be me next."

"No way!" Jared jumped up and the floor shook slightly. His hands were trembling at the same pace as the earth was. He was losing control of his powers. "Nobody is going to get you, I will make sure of that!".

"Calm down, mate," Flint said, releasing Macey's hand to get up. He gripped Jared by the shoulders, shaking him. "You need to snap out of it or we won't have a house anymore."

"I'm still here. He's not going to get me without a fight," she said, trying to fake bravery. She had seen his power. She was no match for him. Waves, none of them were

"So what do we do?" Cam asked, still by her side. "Do we stay here, barricade ourselves in this place, or do we search out whoever wants to harm her?"

Flint sighed. "I think it's time to visit Malan."

"Malan?" she repeated, looking at him with disbelieving eyes, trying to marry up what he was saying now, with what they'd told her before. "But you said that Malan lived centuries ago?" She ended on a short squeak and berated herself inwardly for it. They didn't seem like the type that would be running away now, but she didn't want to take that chance.

"We also told you we'd lived for centuries too," Cam said with a slight laugh. "Is it too far-fetched to think that a prophet's still around too?" She frowned and cocked her head to the side slightly. He had a point, and she wasn't sure she liked that. She really needed to make sure they knew they could be wrong sometimes, it wasn't good to let them know they could be right so often, otherwise she'd end up on the back foot for the rest of her life. Huh, the rest of her life? She glanced at the three men before nodding to herself. The rest of her life didn't seem too bad really. *Damn it, Macey, pull yourself together*, she berated herself. She hadn't known them long enough to be thinking or acting in this way, no matter how right it felt.

"Well, no…"

"And Malan's not exactly around like we are either," Jared added thoughtful, receiving a whack on the arm from Flint.

"Don't spoil the surprise!"

Jared chuckled deeply. "You just want to see her reaction."

"Your point?" Flint smirked and Macey glared at him.

"My reaction to what exactly?" She crossed her arms across her chest, no mean feat considering her position, pushing up her boobs and drawing three sets of eyes. Not her intention admittedly, but she'd take it.

Cam cleared his throat. "To Malan." His voice was husky and he licked his lips, probably subconsciously, but she enjoyed the reaction she got from him. If only now was the time to do something about it.

"What are you hiding?" She narrowed her eyes at Cam, already figuring that he was the one likely to crack first. He looked a little uncomfortable, and couldn't quite meet her gaze, only proving her point more. "Tell me," she hissed. The three men exchanged glances, only worrying her further.

"Malan is..."

"Different?" Jared suggested.

"Dead," Cam supplied.

"How can we talk to him if he's dead?" Macey asked, pulling a confused expression that seemed to have even Flint's expression softening.

"His body is dead, his spirit, not so much. We can still talk to him."

"Cause that makes any sense," Macey muttered, already confused out of her mind.

"So a house in the mists and the Voice in your head are both perfectly acceptable, but talking to someone dead, isn't? Good to know where the boundaries are." Flint's eyes danced with amusement as she looked up into them, and she found she liked this side of him, he seemed a little more angry and serious the rest of the time.

"Talking to the dead does seem a little more extreme," she said, pushing herself up so that she was more upright, and grasping her head as the dull thudding intensified.

"It's really not. We'll visit where his spirit lives, ask him what we want to know, and that's that."

"That's that?!" she half-shouted despite the pain that brought. "Oh hi Macey, what did you do today? Well, I talked to the fucking dead. By the waves, you're all insane." She stood up, swaying slightly with the effort.

"Any more insane than being able to turn into a water horse?" Jared asked, also rising to his feet, with Cam doing the same. The three of them were stood in a circle, with her in the middle. Until she stepped towards Jared that was. She was sure her hair had already begun to turn green, and if the men were to be believed, then her eyes would be glowing too. Miraculously, the headache seemed to have vanished along with her partial shift.

"Call me a water horse again," she challenged Jared, almost feeling her eyes flare and a weird burning sensation on her upper back, but she pushed it all away, not caring what it meant.

"Okay, okay, I'm sorry. You're a kelpie," Jared said, holding up his hands, but still smiling slightly.

"Don't forget it." Her eyes bored into him, and then she fixed an equally stern glare on the other two.

"Wouldn't dream of it," Cam said, shaking his head.

"Not worth it at all," Flint added. "But you need to calm down, Macey. Getting angry isn't going to solve anything."

"Says you!" The laugh she gave sounded a little manic, even to her ears, but that wasn't going to stop her. "You've been nothing but angry since I got here."

"That's not true," Flint said, stepping forward.

"Okay, fine, you've been sixty percent angry since I got here."

Flint laughed, moving closer still so that their bodies were almost touching. "Who counts angry in percentages?" he asked, his voice low and rumbly and tempting. It soothed out some of her anger, and despite herself, she began to calm down, the magic bubbling through her blood almost vanishing completely.

"I do," she insisted, pouting at him.

"It's adorable."

"It is not," she said, putting her hands on her hips and attempting to look stern. Though that was well and truly undermined by the effect his closeness was having on her. Really, all she wanted was to press her body against his and let him kiss her. Maybe Jared's magic had taken hold of her again, that could explain why she was suddenly thinking with parts a lot lower down than her brain. Stupid men, distracting her with their sexiness.

"Oh, it is Macey." He cupped her cheek in his hand in a surprisingly gentle gesture, before leaning down and pressing a swift kiss to her lips. He pulled back, his eyes meeting hers, and while she could see the desire burning within them, she knew he wouldn't go any further right now. He'd decided on the next step, and she suspected that nothing she could say or do would change that.

"Let me just break this sexual tension by saying that we should really leave if we want to see Malan today," Jared said and Macey was tempted to strangle him. Not just because he mentioned sexual tension. Also because he was right.

"How do we get there?" she asked, stepping out of the circle and rummaging through the clothes Flint must have brought with him. What did someone wear when they went to visit a ghost? Black? Or would that be too morbid?

"The Staran, if they let us leave," Cam explained, looking a little doubtful. If it hadn't let him leave earlier, it might not now. But this time, it was important.

Macey put on a black hoodie over her top - just to be on the safe side - and slipped on her boots. "I'm ready. Shall we go?"

She strode out of the room, the guys' chuckles following her. She didn't quite understand what they found so funny, but they were guys, so she didn't even try to. They rarely made sense; it had been the same thing underwater. The number of times she had struggled to grasp why her brothers did things... no, she didn't want to think about her brothers. They were either victims, or evil bastards, and somehow nobody could tell her which option was correct. Maybe the dead guy could tell them. Malan.

She waited by the door until the three men joined her. Flint was wearing a big backpack. When he saw her questioning glance, he shrugged. "Malan likes gifts, and he likely won't talk if we don't bring him anything."

"Are you all ready? We might run into trouble," Cam said. Jared grinned and opened his jacket wide, exposing a row of throwing stars attached to the lining. Flint produced a silver lighter from his breast pocket and flicked it on, smiling at the flame.

"Why do you need a lighter?" Macey asked, and he winked.

"Because it looks cool."

She rolled her eyes and turned to Cam. "Do I need anything? And if you ask if I have a trident, I'm going to kill you, slowly."

"I wasn't going to ask that... But I'm sure you'd

look hot with it," he smirked and left the house, disappearing into the mists.

She followed, flanked by the other two guys. The fog was thick, almost touchable. Macey had never seen anything like it before - if she ignored the night of her kidnapping. It was unnatural, no, it was supernatural.

"It's just a two-minute walk to the Staran," Cam called from in front of her, but it came as a whisper, the mist swallowing every sound. Following his voice, she walked slowly, careful not to trip. She couldn't even see her feet, but it felt like she was walking on gravel.

"How about a stopover on Earth?" Jared shouted. "Malan likes those Belgian waffles, we should probably get him some."

"I want some too!" Flint chimed in. Macey noticed how hungry she was. Waffles sounded like a great idea. Much more appealing than walking through this strange mist.

She bumped into Cam with a yelp. Why couldn't he have warned her that he stopped walking? That wasn't an unreasonable request in this weather, was it?

"We're here," he explained, taking her hand.

She looked around, but all she could see was fog. This spot wasn't any less misty than the last couple hundred yards.

"How do you know?" she asked and he sighed.

"I don't know. Jared's been asking me for years, but I... just know. Same as Flint. We can always feel where the doorways to the Staran are. And this one here is a good one. That's probably why they built the house here."

She frowned. "They? Isn't it your house?"

"Oh no, it's been here for millenia. No idea who built it originally. It changes over time, and sometimes new rooms appear when we need them. Our entertainment room only appeared two years ago, but I guess the game consoles weren't as good before that."

"So your house is magical?"

"I guess." He shrugged as if it wasn't a big deal, while Macey was having trouble getting her head around it. A house that added new rooms. Maybe she could ask it for a hot tub? Or a painting studio? She'd always loved to paint, even though the techniques underwater were very different from those humans used.

"You need to hold onto me and don't let go no matter what happens," Cam explained. "Flint will take Jared."

"But I wanted to take Macey!" Flint complained. "She's much more fun than Earth guy."

"Then you should have claimed her first," Cam snarled, his humour suddenly gone. Macey stared at him wide-eyed, not quite sure whether he was only talking about travelling through the Mists. It didn't seem like it... and in her mind, she had already claimed them. Not just Cam. All of them. They were hers. She grimaced at the thought of anyone else taking them. No way. She just hoped the other three elements wouldn't turn out to be girls. Unless they weren't into men, of course.

"Could we get out of this mist?" She tried to diffuse the tension. "This stuff is getting my clothes wet."

Cam pulled her close and wrapped her into his arms. She didn't mind travelling through the Staran. They should do this more often. She liked being in his arms, warm and cosy. Although it would be more fun if they weren't wearing as many clothes...

"Ready?" Cam called and the others all confirmed.

Macey was getting a little jitterish. The last time Cam had transported her on the Staran, she'd been unconscious. Would it hurt? Be uncomfortable?

A tight squeeze was all the warning she got before they plunged into nothingness.

Darkness.

No, not darkness.

Nothing.

No light.

No dark.

No shadows.

Just her and Cam, their bodies united, being thrown through the universe.

It was hard to focus, but she tried to think about however Cam would know where to stop. Where to get out of this vacuum. If they could get out of it. Maybe it had all gone terribly wrong? Maybe this wasn't the Staran?

A pain around her navel area made her scream as they were pulled backwards as if ropes were attached to their bellies. Suddenly there was darkness, and pain, so much pain, agony, never-ending agon-

Solid ground appeared beneath their feet and they stumbled forwards before collapsing on the ground. Shaking from top to feet, Macey looked around. They were in the Mists again. She couldn't see the house, so wasn't sure if they'd returned to the place they'd started from.

"Guess we still can't get to Earth," Cam groaned, releasing her from his grip. A second later, Jared and Flint appeared out of nowhere, falling before they could get their balance. "And neither can they."

Na Fir Ghorma (Blue Men of the Minch)

8

"What the fuck are those?" she half-screamed, staring at the blue man-shaped things that seemed to be staring at the four of them.

"They're *na fir ghorma*," Cam replied, his voice shaking ever so slightly. So that wasn't good. Not in the slightest.

"Storm kelpies? I'm telling you, those aren't kelpies." She took an involuntary step backwards, colliding with someone's chest. Jared's she guessed, he wasn't as warm as Flint was, and Cam was stood to her right.

"I don't think the *na fir ghorma* are actual kelpies, Macey," Jared added.

"No shit." She looked the blue men up and down. They were certainly odd looking, and they did appear as if they came from the water. They even had webbed hands which would've made swimming easy. But then, what the heck were they doing here?

"So what do they do?" Flint asked, and she whipped her head around to look at him, shocked that he didn't know. Even in the short time she'd known him, he'd been the most knowledgeable of the three of them.

"Erm, call storms, I think," Cam stuttered. If storms were all they had to worry about, she didn't know why he was so shaken.

"And?" she prompted.

"No one is really sure, they're supposedly descended from fallen angels."

Macey snorted. "Angels don't exist."

"You sound very certain about that for someone who's something that shouldn't exist too," Jared pointed out.

"Not true. Kelpies are obviously real. Gods, heaven, and angels are not." She pulled away from him.

"How do you really know that though?" Jared questioned.

"I just do," she snapped, the magic already bubbling up inside her.

"Question is, what are they doing here?" Cam asked quietly, almost as if talking to himself.

"Walking towards us," Macey deadpanned, trying not to sound too concerned, despite the hoard of blueness coming their way with gormless expressions on their faces. They kind of reminded her of the zombies in the stupid horror films her brothers had made her watch.

"I don't mean that, I mean why are they away from the Minch." He tapped his chin as if lost in thought. She did have to question *why* he thought now was a good time to start thinking about these things. Maybe later, once they'd decided what to do about them, and had done it, he could muse on the reasons behind it.

"The Minch being..."

"Oh you're such a loch kelpie," Cam teased, his expression lightening for a moment. Macey growled. All kelpies lived in lochs, there was no need for him to make it sound like he was some kind of lesser being because of it. Seeming to sense her anger, Cam held up his hands. "Meant nothing by it, Mace. The Minch is a straight of sea between the Hebrides and the Highlands." She nodded, remembering where he meant from the map of Scotland she'd studied shortly after coming to land.

"Which answers none of the pressing questions. Like where are we? Why the fuck are there blue men making their way towards us? Or, you know, what are we going to do about it?" Flint sounded half-amused, half-serious, for which Macey was glad, and not just because it seemed to relax Cam a bit. He definitely seemed less on edge than before.

"Well I suspect we're in the Staran above the Minch," Cam suggested.

"So they're supposed to be here then?" Jared asked.

"Erm...I'm going to go with no," Cam said, looking towards the men again. Macey followed his gaze before sucking in a worried breath. That didn't bode well at all. Several of the *na fir ghorma* had opened their mouths about three times as wide as they should be able to, which was freaky to say the least, a little terrifying at worst. Even from afar she could see sharp teeth protruding from their extended jaws. Scary. Especially given the clouds that seemed to be swirling above them. Which was odd in itself. Why were there clouds above the mists? That wasn't normal she was sure.

"What do they want from us?" Macey stammered slightly, inwardly hating that she was showing such weakness in front of the three of them.

"How should I know, I haven't exactly gone up and had a chat with them." She was a little taken aback by Cam's sarcasm. He'd never come across like that before. Her initial instinct was to snap at him, but really, that wasn't going to get them anywhere.

"Can Flint burn them away?"

"Burn them?" the man in question asked.

"Yes, burn them. You can create flames, right?" He nodded in response to her question and lifted a hand, a small ball of orange flames hovering above it.

"I can, but that's not exactly how attacking a water being works."

"Oh." Well, that was her out of ideas. Or was it? "What about another water being?" she asked cautiously.

"I honestly don't know," Cam answered. "But considering they're getting closer by the second, I'd suggest we stop talking about it and actually do something." Despite knowing that now really wasn't the time, she found herself admiring this side of Cam. This Cam was a leader, which was an interesting switch considering it had been Flint who took the lead the most in the house.

"Okay," she admitted, and widened her stance, noting that the three men joined her in a line, Flint to her left, Jared to her right, and Cam next to him. She wasn't exactly sure what they were going to do, but just standing there as a united front was enough for her.

"Can you even use magic again?" Jared asked.

"I don't know," she said honestly. "But I guess we're about to find out." She concentrated on the water that bubbled in her blood and began to draw it to the surface. As she did, a chill wind began to whip around her, and one glance to her right and Cam's outstretched hands confirmed her suspicions that it was him calling it.

Strands of green hair flickered in front of her eyes. By the waves, she really should have thought to tie her hair back. Rule 101 of getting into a fight: make sure hair was tied back. It was a rookie error really.

We are not here to fight.

A voice suddenly whispered in Macey's head, faint as the wind. She looked at her companions and their startled expressions confirmed that they had heard it too.

"They certainly look like they're about to attack," she mumbled under her breath. "Do you think it's a ploy to lower our guard?"

"No idea, but it would be wrong to attack them now. Let's stay vigilant, but we won't be the ones to start a fight," Cam whispered back.

Macey nodded and waved at the blue men. One of them - a large guy with a massive sapphire mane - stepped forward and imitated her gesture.

"What do you want?" she shouted, hoping they could hear her through the mist. It had become a little less foggy now, and she was able to make out more and more detail of their strange surroundings. They seemed to be standing on a frozen loch, or river, or... some frozen body of water. A thin layer of frost covered the ice, forming strange patterns that looked like they weren't just random.

We need help.

"Join the club," Flint sighed.

"Maybe they can help us get waffles if we help them in return?" Jared asked hopefully and Macey had to hide a grin. This maybe wasn't the best time for Jared's sense of humour.

"How can we help?" she shouted, having taken on the role of negotiator. She was used to it; letting her help in resolving arguments had been one of her father's strategies. People were more likely to give an innocent looking girl what she wanted than a king.

The Storms are in uproar. They told us to find the Seven Wardens. We asked the Staran to take us to them. Now we're here. But there are only four of you.

Macey grimaced. Yes, they were working on that. Not that she fully believed in the whole Warden thingy. It was a little too far-fetched, even for a kelpie.

"How can the Wardens help you?" she asked.

The blue men's leader did something like a shrug, but it didn't quite work. It was clear they weren't used to being out of the water.

The Storms will know. You need to come with us.

"Sorry, we're kind of busy right now!" Flint shouted before she could reply. "I don't trust them," he whispered. "It's all too much of a coincidence that they found us here. We need to get to Malan, he will have some answers. I hope."

"What if he doesn't?" Macey asked.

"Then we can visit the *na fir ghorma?*" He smiled sheepishly, seeing the flaw in his argument. They had no idea how to get to the blue men, nor where exactly they lived. The Minch was a large area.

"We will come with you!" Macey called to the groan of the guys.

"Who put you in charge?" Jared complained. "I wanted waffles."

"Are there any other princesses amongst us? No? See, I'm the only one. I outrank you."

"I'm not a kelpie," he began to argue, but she cut him off by walking towards the blue men.

"Do you promise us safe passage?" she asked, feeling very important. This was like something that happened in books.

Of course. You will each have to hold hands with us. The Staran won't let you enter our kingdom otherwise.

"Oh, you've got a monarchy as well?" She was beginning to see similarities between the two kelpie kinds.

Yes. I am Muahwa, the Crown Prince. Take my hand.

She looked at his outstretched, webbed, slightly slimy hand. By the waves, she hadn't expected to touch a merman when she woke up this morning. Although he might eat her if he knew she was calling him that. What else were those giant mouths for if not to eat people? They seemed to talk with their minds only; none of them had uttered a single word since they'd appeared.

Nodding at her companions to do the same, she put her hand in his, surprised at the warmth of his skin. They each chose a blue man to touch... okay, that sounded strange. Creepy.

Ready?

Before she could nod, they were pulled into the nothingness of the Staran once more.

THE NOTHINGNESS HAPPENED AGAIN. Though at least this time she was ready for it. Almost. The painful tug in her stomach didn't happen this time either, which confirmed that they'd been pulled out of the Staran early last time. Or at least, it did in Macey's mind; Cam and Flint may end up feeling different.

She looked around, surprised to find herself standing inside what appeared to be half a bubble surrounded by water. She shuddered. It felt unnatural, she shouldn't be in human form while surrounded by water. How was she supposed to breathe? Or swim?

Okay, she knew how she'd swim, she was just as

capable of swimming in human form as she was when a full kelpie, but that wasn't the point.

"I don't like this," Flint murmured from behind her, and she could sense his uneasiness. She let go of the hand of the blue prince and turned to meet his worried eyes. His fire seemed dimmer than before and she wondered why. Until she began cursing herself, that was. How hadn't she realised that being underwater, even if it was in a bubble of air, would be uncomfortable for someone whose whole body was filled with fire?

Instead of saying anything, she slipped her hand into Flint's and squeezed. He returned the gesture, a weak smile flitting over his face.

"I thought you floated on the top of the water?" Cam asked shortly after arriving himself, with Jared and his *na fir ghorma*.

We used to, but now the humans are too many.

"Ah."

It is safer to live beneath the seas and surface only at night.

"For you maybe," Flint muttered darkly.

You're perfectly safe Flame-Man. Nothing has broken through our dome since we created it.

"Why do you even have a dome?" Macey asked, still slightly in awe of her surroundings. She looked up, watching as marine life went on above the dome. A shadow passed overhead, swinging its tail from side to side in a graceful movement. Well, she never thought she'd see a shark swimming above her head. Or at least, not one that wasn't in an aquarium. She shivered slightly, wondering what else was real, and suddenly feeling like she *was* a sheltered loch kelpie. No wonder her people traditionally went on quests, there was so much more to life than their one loch.

We need air as well as water. Our ancestors discovered this way of getting both.

"But I don't feel wet," Jared said, stepping up behind Macey and stroking her back gently. If he carried on doing that, then she certainly would be.

The air is filled with what we need. The salt and the essence. It gives us what we need while still allowing us to breathe.

"I'm so reassured."

"Flint!" Macey scolded, mortified by his sarcasm. They were guests. Instead, the *na fir ghorma* Prince seemed to chuckle, his shoulders lifting up and down as he did, but no real sound coming out, nor did it appear in his mind.

I feel the same on land Flame-Man. But I promise you are safe.

"Thank you," Macey answered hastily, before Flint or one of her other men spoke without thinking and ruined a good thing.

We'll be having a feast in your honour this evening, I'll have some clothing sent to your room.

"Room?" Macey squeaked, causing Flint to squeeze her hand this time, and Jared to press his hand more firmly against her back.

Yes, room. You are the Wardens, correct?

"I...yes," she answered, realising that denying it wouldn't do them much good right at this moment.

Then I will take you to your room.

9

If you ignored that the bedroom had a glass ceiling that looked out into the ocean, it wasn't all that different from a house on Earth. With the exception that it was rare to find a bedroom with seven large beds. Was that just coincidence or connected to the Seven Wardens?

Macey was a little apprehensive about it all. It seemed like the blue men had high expectations for them. And she knew absolutely nothing about the prophecy, or what it had to do with her.

Jared threw himself onto one of the beds and spread out his arms. "I like this place. My bed at home isn't as wide."

Cam tsked and looked around, examining the room for threats - at least that's what it looked like.

Flint took Macey's hand and pulled her towards him until she was in his arms, hugged close.

"Are you okay?" he asked in his deep, gentle voice that sounded like embers in a hot fire.

She was about to ask why she wouldn't be, but that might destroy the atmosphere. So she just nodded and snuggled against his broad chest. He was so nice and warm... Maybe she could persuade him to lie down on the bed? Together? Cuddling? Maybe more? And maybe the other two could join them?

A knock on the door destroyed her fantasies and she stepped away from Flint. They had to keep up appearances, after all.

A young woman entered - the first female *na fir ghorma* she had seen so far. She didn't look much different though: the same large mouth, seaweed-like hair, webbed hands and bluish skin. The main thing giving away her gender were the massive breasts, covered only by two seashells. Macey gulped. Hopefully, her guys weren't into blue-boobed girls. Size wasn't everything, right?

Again she noticed how in her mind, she had claimed them as hers. Which was slightly preposterous, given that she had yet to kiss one of them. And her incubus-induced kiss with Cam probably didn't count either. Which meant she'd only kissed Flint, twice. Maybe she should focus on one of them for now instead of all three? But then she thought of funny Jared who tortured himself by not feeding, and Cam, who was still feeling guilty for kidnapping her.

"The cook wants to know what you want for dinner," the blue woman asked. "We don't know what Wardens eat."

"We're not Wardens," Macey began, but Cam cut her off.

"We like our fish cooked, if that's possible. Otherwise, we should be able to eat anything you eat."

Macey hoped that was true. Who knew what these people here ate. She was aware that she might be a little prejudiced, but she was a kelpie and found these people calling themselves storm kelpies an insult to her people. They didn't even have hooves.

"Cooked fish? But that takes away all the flavour," the woman stuttered, obviously confused. "We only cook kelp to make it softer. But I will pass your wishes on to the kitchen." With a look of disdain on her face, she left.

"How do you eat your fish?" Cam asked Macey and she grimaced.

"We don't eat fish. Do you eat your pets?" He shook his head. "See? We don't, either."

"You keep fish as pets?" Jared gave her a doubtful look as if he wasn't sure whether she was joking or not.

"Of course, I had several as a child. And a lobster named Clawy."

Jared started laughing, but she ignored him.

"Kelpies are vegetarians, didn't you know? I only started eating meat when I came to live on land, but even now, I don't eat it very often. All those animals are... weird. They don't live in water."

Now Jared was close to choking, his face flushed.

"You're very cute," Flint whispered, his breath hot on her neck. He gently took her shoulders and turned her around until she was looking at him. His eyes were like smouldering coals, waiting to warm her. Or burn her, if she wasn't careful. She knew that Flint didn't do things halfway. If she gave herself to him, he would take all of her and more. He was intense like that. Like the fire, his element.

He bent down and gave her a chaste kiss on the forehead. Her nipples stiffened as the touch of his lips sent sparks through her body. How could one tiny kiss have that effect on her?

He cupped her face and trailed a row of soft kisses down her cheek, then her chin, ignoring her mouth. Damn that guy, teasing her like that. She shivered when he reached her throat.

"Would you two lovebirds please stop? We need to talk strategy," Cam complained, but when Macey turned around, she could see the jealousy in his eyes. Damn, she wanted to run over to him and kiss him.

Fuck it.

She did it.

She had to stand on her toes to reach him, but he responded immediately, opening his mouth to let her in. She found his tongue with her own and gently let him know that she was here for him. Not just for Flint. For them all.

She broke the kiss and just stared into his eyes, acutely aware of both of their laboured breathing, and the weight of his hands on her hips. He wasn't as warm as Flint was, but there was still a comfort in the strength of his touch.

"I see how it is," Jared said, but she didn't turn to look at him. She didn't need to, she could hear from his voice that he was only playing. "All the kisses for Cam and Flint, and none for me?"

"Maybe if you sounded less pouty," she suggested, pulling away from Cam so she could turn to look at him. Jared's dark gaze bore into her, his eyes filled with lust. But this lust was different from the night before. She wasn't sure exactly how she knew that, but she did.

He reached out and pulled Macey towards him, not too roughly, but with enough force for her to know he was claiming her. Good. She wanted them all to claim her, just like she had them. He crushed his lips to hers, passionate and sure, branding her as his own. She just hoped he'd learn to share. No way was she letting Flint and Cam go too.

She pressed her body into his, revelling in how well their bodies fit together. Thought fled, and the only thing she could focus on was the hand he'd tangled in her hair, tugging ever so slightly, and the other that held her firmly to his chest. Her nipples peaked beneath the thin material of her shirt as they rubbed against his chest. Macey moaned into his mouth, lost in the moment. Jared ended the kiss, staring down at her with promise in his eyes.

"We should go see where the fish has got to," Flint muttered.

"Do we have to?" Cam almost whined, but Macey ignored him, only having eyes for Jared. She wanted the other two. Oh, how she wanted them, but something told her that Jared needed her the most.

"Yes, this time." Flint's tone dripped with promise, one she hoped he'd fulfil later. But he was right, this time wasn't for them.

"Fine. But next time..."

"Yes, you can monopolise Macey next time," Flint said with an unhappy side. Something inside her whinnied, pleased that he wanted her so much. But not now. Now, she only had eyes for Jared.

"Just go," Jared growled, making Macey's skin tingle. There was raw power in his words, power that no one could deny, and she wondered if it was part of his incubus magic, or if it was just something more him than that. She heard Cam and Flint leave the room and smiled, until she saw the serious look on Jared's face. "Take your clothes off." He looked deadly serious, his eyes burning into her, and igniting her in a way even Flint didn't.

Anticipation built within her as she stripped herself of her shirt and jeans, dropping them to the floor and leaving her bared to him in just her underwear. Despite the openness of the room, she didn't feel exposed though. Not at all. Instead, Macey felt electrified. Her blood sizzled and she was about ready to beg for his touch if it didn't come soon.

He circled her slowly, almost close enough to touch, but not quite. Macey whimpered. He needed to touch her soon. He had to. If he didn't, she'd melt into a pile of need and might never surface again.

"Please," she whispered hoarsely. She hadn't meant to let him know quite how desperate she was right at this moment, but it was too late for that now. Jared chuckled.

"Please what, Macey?" he almost purred her name as he stepped up behind her. She could feel his warmth against her back. And yet he was still holding back.

"Touch me," she begged.

"Not yet." Macey could hear the amusement in

his tone, and if she hadn't been able to pick up the slight undercurrent of something else too, then she might have been mad.

They stood unmoving for another few moments, the anticipation between them almost being too much. When it became clear he wasn't going to make the first move, she turned swiftly and pressed her body against his. Macey raised herself on tip toes so she could capture his mouth with hers.

There was nothing gentle about this kiss either. It was intense. It was powerful, and it was everything that she needed right at this moment. Maybe she shouldn't be kissing one of the men who'd effectively kidnapped her and held her to ransom, but she pushed the thought away quickly. If they'd wanted to take advantage of her, then they could have done while she was under Jared's magic the first time. Well, the only time. She was definitely under his spell right now, but it was a spell of a different kind.

Jared's strong hands lifted her so that she could wrap her legs around his waist without losing the connection between them. Once she was settled, he made this way over to the bed, and Macey tried her best not to rub against him too much as he walked. Getting there was by far the most important thing right now.

He pulled away and looked at her with a tender expression on his face, before dropping her down onto the bed and pulling his shirt over his head. Macey propped herself up on her elbows, watching intently as he revealed his toned chest. She licked her lips, anxious for him to reveal more.

Jared's hands rested on his fly, but he didn't make any move to take off the rest of his clothing. Instead, he grinned at Macey knowingly and nodded towards her.

"Oh," she said, scrambling slightly to remove what remained of her own clothes, not giving a second thought to how exposed that would make her. He'd already seen her naked after all, this was no different. Plus, it wasn't exactly the same for her, not with her having to be naked to shift all the time, and her kelpie form didn't wear clothing anyway.

She lay back down on the bed and watched as Jared finally pushed down his jeans, revealing what she really wanted to see. Her mouth went dry, and while she wanted to demand he join her, she couldn't find a way to actually form the words. Luckily, she didn't seem to need to, as the bed dipped down when Jared settled in beside her.

Gently, he trailed a finger down her cheek, drawing her mouth to his in a kiss that was completely different to their previous ones. It was softer, with a soft edge to it that conveyed that this was far more than just about the physical. It was odd how she knew that. She hadn't known him long, and yet this felt so right.

Jared's free hand trailed across her skin, leaving tingles in its wake and making her hot with need. He seemed to sense it, and moved his hand inwards, so that his fingers brushed across the sensitive skin of her inner thighs, making her shiver. She opened her legs wider, hoping he got the hint without them having to end the kiss so she could tell him to hurry the fuck up.

The moment he slipped a first finger into her, she let out a loud moan, ending the kiss she'd been anxious not to just seconds before. He gave her a self-satisfied smile before adding a second. By the waves, it was like nothing else before. Something began to mount inside her, spreading through her like the pull of water before a tsunami hit.

"Jared," she moaned.

"Yes, Macey?" He sounded almost as breathless as she did, even though she wasn't doing anything to him, which only wound her up tighter.

"More," she just about managed to get out through her erratic breathing. He didn't say anything, just increased the rhythm in which he moved, leaning in to trail a path of kisses down her neck. He nibbled gently, and that was all it took for everything to unlock, and a wave of pleasure to course through her.

She arched off the bed, shuddering and unable to control the noises she was making.

After a few moments, the intensity subsided, and she collapsed back onto the bed, spent and wanting more. Her eyes met Jared's and she smiled at him.

"Did you know your hair's green?" he asked, brushing a stray lock away from her face as he did.

"It is?" she asked weakly.

"Yes. But it's fading now." She couldn't quite describe the look on his face, but then again, she could barely form a coherent sentence in her head, so that wasn't all that surprising really.

"Oh."

"Anger and orgasms turn your hair green. Good to know." He chuckled and dropped a quick kiss on her lips. "Want to see if we can do it again?" He smirked at her knowingly, and she wrapped her arms around his neck, pulling him closer so that she could kiss him again and tell him without words that more was exactly what she wanted.

"Did you know that you're sparkling?" she whispered as he broke their kiss to take a deep breath. "Just like vampires."

"Vampires don't sparkle." He looked down on himself. "And neither do I."

"But they do, I read it in a book. And not your body, silly, but your eyes." She gently stroked his cheek with her thumb, staring into his dark, sparkly eyes. "It's like you have a whole little universe in there. Lots of stars."

"Are you alright? Did I break you somehow?" He chuckled and began to adjust himself over her. She felt him at her entrance and spread her legs even wider in anticipation. Feeling his fingers had been amazing, but now she was ready for the real thing. Sparkling or not.

"Do it," she moaned as he kissed her gently.

"Say please," he whispered hoarsely.

"Please, Jared." Hearing herself so desperate and needy made her feel even more turned on.

"Hold on tight, little kelpie. You've never had an incubus before, but I'm going to show you why we are desired by every female on this planet." She was probably supposed to laugh at that grandiose statement, but right in that moment, he pushed inside her and she forgot whatever she had been thinking. Bliss and a slight tinge of pain were all she could feel. He was everything.

She screamed as he began to move in her, wrapping her legs around him to pull him closer. Deeper. He was filling something deep inside her that she hadn't realised had been empty. Not physically... although he was filling her in that way too... but no, it was different. Like a piece of a puzzle that had been lost and was now finally being added. And it fit perfectly. Only... it felt like other pieces were missing too. Strange.

He pulled her up without warning until she was sitting on his thighs, him still inside her.

"Does that feel good?" he asked, almost as if he wasn't quite sure.

"Yes, and now continue, you silly incubus," she moaned, grinding on his lap to convey the message.

"Is my kelpie getting sassy?" he whispered, his voice pure seduction. "I may have to punish you for that."

"Then do it," she screamed as he pulled her down on him, hard, while pressing upwards at the same time. He was deeper than he had been before, pushing her further towards ecstasy. She was so close, but he had stopped moving, apparently enjoying this torture.

"Please," she moaned again, "don't stop now."

"I think we need a break," he quipped and pulled out of her, lowering her back onto the bed. She was lying there, speechless, the emptiness in her almost painful. She needed him to fill it again. She needed him to make her feel good. Make her come, like before.

Instead, he was standing at the edge of the bed, naked and hard, watching her.

"What the fucking waves are you doing?" she whimpered, her hands moving between her legs without her doing. She needed to find completion.

"Don't touch yourself," Jared commanded and to her own surprise, she stopped. "Now turn and lie on your belly."

She did as he asked, again without thinking. He was in full incubus mode now and she accepted that he had a power over her other men wouldn't. She enjoyed it, actually.

He walked around the bed until he was standing on one side. She turned her head and looked straight at his erection. Had he really been inside her? How the waves had he been able to fit?

She wasn't sure if she'd be allowed to touch him, so she waited, lying on the bed obediently. This was new territory for her. Usually, she was the one who had control.

A gentle touch on her back made her shiver. Jared was trailing one finger down her body, slowly getting closer to where she wanted him to be. He drew a circle on her bum and she moaned in frustration. He laughed. "Do you want more, little one?"

"Yes, please," she whispered, her voice threatening to fail.

Suddenly, he slapped her arse and she cried out in surprise. Nobody had ever done that before. But she had to admit, now that the sharp pain was giving way to pleasure... she liked it.

He bent forward and gently licked the skin he had just decorated with a red handprint. Her skin was incredibly sensitive, even just a normal handshake left it flushed. She imagined his mark on her, the sign he had claimed her. She got even wetter at that thought.

Without warning, he slapped her other cheek and this time, her cry became a moan.

"So you like that, little kelpie?"

"Yes!" she groaned, arching her back so he had better access to her arse. He chuckled and once again licked her skin. This time, he didn't stop and slowly made his way down until he reached her core. She whimpered as his tongue touched that tiny point of pleasure that made her shiver in anticipation. She needed him, more, now!

"Fuck me," she moaned and was rewarded with another slap.

"Are you telling me what to do?" His voice had grown harsh, but still playful.

"Yes. No. I don't know," she whispered. "I need more, please."

"Spread your legs," he commanded and joined her on the large bed. She did as he asked and was rewarded with a finger entering her from behind. She hoped this was just the vanguard, a promise of more to come.

And she was right. A second later, his finger was replaced by something a lot larger as he entered her in one long, hard push.

She gripped the bed sheets tightly as he began to

fuck her fast and rough. There was no holding back now. Her moans grew louder and his heavy breathing joined their song.

When she came, he did it as well, uniting them in a rush of pleasure that took them far away from the glass-domed chamber they were in.

10

"What did you do to her?" Flint asked, amusement filling his tone. He wasn't mad then. Or at least as far as Macey's sleep-addled brain could tell. Oh. She'd fallen asleep; apparently, good sex did that to her. No, not good sex. Great sex. With an incubus. Did that mean he owned her soul now? She'd admit to having no clue how incubi worked. Though the other question was whether she cared if he did. Worryingly, she didn't seem to mind the idea of losing her soul to him. Or the others. She pushed the hazy thought away. She'd deal with it when she was properly awake.

"Took her to heaven."

"Seems unlikely. You're the son of a demon," Cam pointed out, and even in her sleepy frame of mind, she wanted to laugh.

"That's just how good I am." Macey could hear the smirk in his voice, but couldn't really dispute his words.

"No such thing as heaven," she murmured, and Jared chuckled, sounding closer than he had before.

"Is there not, little one?" Heat flooded through her as she remembered the last time he'd called her that. But she wouldn't let that distract her. At least, not too much.

"No," she said, blinking a few times and finally opening her eyes fully. Jared was sitting near her on the bed, a caring look on his face which was quickly replaced with a wicked smile.

"Then I don't know how to describe being inside you."

She swallowed almost audibly, aware of Flint and Cam's eyes on her, as well as her current state of nakedness. She glanced at them, noting the hunger in their eyes instantly. A thrill shot through her. If they were okay with knowing Jared had already had her, and willing to do the same, then she was going to be a very happy kelpie.

"What time is it?" she asked, despite that not being the real question she wanted to ask. That question would end with them on the bed too. Or she hoped it would.

"Not time for that," Flint said firmly. "It's almost time to go to the feast."

Macey groaned. How had she forgotten about that? Oh yes. A well-endowed incubus doing things to her body that she hadn't imagined possible. Anyone would forget about a stupid feast then.

"Do we have to?" she whined.

"Yes," Cam replied. "And they've sent you something to wear." He sounded both amused and uneasy.

He handed her a small fabric bundle and she sat up to take a closer look. It seemed too small to be clothes. Maybe a t-shirt, or a small skirt. But then with a shudder, she remembered the blue girl from earlier and how she hadn't worn a lot of clothes. Except that for her, it wasn't as obvious with her colourful skin and scales. But Macey was very pale and didn't like being exposed in front of a group of creepy blue men.

With a sigh, she unwrapped the bundle and held up the tiny dress inside. 'Dress' was an overstatement. Think dishcloth around the bum with a strap to kind of cover her boobs. And even the sparse fabric that was there didn't hide anything. It was sheer. Who the waves came up with this monstrosity? She could just as well go there naked.

"I told them you wouldn't like it," Cam said, visibly uncomfortable. Macey wasn't going to shoot the messenger. No, she was going to shoot the designer.

"I'm not going to wear this," she stated and the

three guys groaned. "I'm going in my normal clothes, and if they don't like it, to hell with them."

Jared grinned. "You said there is no hell."

"Right now, there is," she grumbled. "It's the only place this dress can have come from."

"It's not that bad," Cam tried to appease her. "Maybe put in on, just for us?"

She sighed, but then remembered she wasn't wearing anything right now. This dress would actually be an improvement.

Trying to wiggle her hips seductively (maybe there was still a chance to spend the evening in bed rather than at the feast) she climbed out of the bed, ignoring the hungry glances the guys tried to hide.

"What's that on your shoulder?" Flint suddenly asked, destroying the effect she had hoped for.

"What?" She craned her head, trying to see what he and the others were looking at. "I can't see it? Are you messing with me?"

"No... Did you always have a tattoo on your shoulder?" Cam asked carefully, drawing a finger over her shoulder blade.

"I don't have a tattoo. I'm scared of needles." It was so bad that she almost fainted when she saw one of her brothers getting tattooed once.

"Well, you certainly have one now," Cam muttered, still touching her skin.

"No, I don't."

"You do - look in the mirror."

She sighed and walked over to the full-length mirror next to the closet. She gasped. There was indeed a tattoo on her shoulder. It was a brown colour, not much darker than her skin; a circle that turned into a spiral. It reminded her of a Celtic symbol. But what the heck was it doing on her skin? She definitely hadn't been to a tattoo parlour recently. All she had done...

"Jared! What did you do?" She turned and prowled towards him, not caring that she was naked. He held up his hands in mock defence.

"Nothing. I swear, nobody I've ever slept with woke up with a tattoo the morning after. It's not what incubi do."

"But it's there!" She was becoming slightly hysteric now. Not because it was an ugly mark - not at all, it was actually really pretty - but because she didn't have a choice about it. If they ended up in bed again, would she get another one? She shuddered at the thought. She'd be covered in ink soon.

"Calm down. Let's just forget about it for now and get ready for the feast?" Cam was trying to be the voice of reason as always. She wanted to snap at him, but he was right. This was something to worry about later.

"Let's try this thing on," she muttered and held the dress in front of her, trying to find the best way to get it onto her body without ripping anything. This was definitely a no-bra and no-panties kind of dress.

"What do you think?" she asked when she finally had it on.

Silence. Then Cam cleared his throat. "It looks good."

"Seriously? That's all you have to say? I guess I better put on my normal clothes after all."

"Don't!" Flint immediately said, even going as far as putting himself between her and her jeans. "I want to be able to look at you all evening like this. You're exquisite."

"But surely I look naked?" she asked, looking down at herself, her barely covered belly, her definitely not covered legs.

Jared chuckled and stepped forward, cupping her face and pulling her towards him. "Yes, you do. But that's what we like about it." He kissed her gently; very different from his claiming kisses earlier that day. She wrapped her arms around him and leaned into the kiss, her body fitting his perfectly.

A knock at the door made her growl. "I don't want to go," she moaned, "there are so many better things we could do."

"We are the Wardens. We have responsibilities," Cam said, suddenly serious. "But I promise you, I'm going to personally take this dress off you tonight."

She sighed. "Let's do this."

They followed a young blue man through the underwater city. Macey couldn't stop looking up at the glass ceilings, watching in awe as a pod of porpoises swam past. They didn't have those in the loch she'd grown up in. She was tempted to shift into her kelpie form and go for a swim with them. But there was that pesky feast to endure.

She'd always hated official celebrations. Her father did a lot of those each year, and as the only girl in the family, she had to sit on his side, separated from her brothers on his other. All the other kelpies her age were sitting far away from her, and it was as boring as kelp. So yeah, she wasn't looking forward to yet another feast.

The blue man opened two large, shell-encrusted doors and Macey couldn't help but stare. There were hundreds of *na fir ghorma* sitting at long rows of tables. She never thought there were that many of them. They were mostly males, but she could spot a few women in between. Most of them were wearing even less than she was.

It felt like hundreds of eyes bored into her and the others as they entered the room. Probably because that's exactly what was happening. She supposed that in their position she'd have been just as curious, especially if she believed what they were saying about them being the Wardens. Macey still had her doubts, but while they were being treated well, she wasn't going to voice them aloud. Plus, it meant that she got to share a room with all three of the very sexy men who seemed to have claimed her as their own. They'd soon find that she was the one doing the claiming.

They walked between two of the long tables, being led towards the high table at which there were several empty seats. For them she assumed. Yet another perk of being a Warden, maybe? She just hoped that they didn't try to make her eat fish. Other meat on land was bad enough, but fish was just wrong. She'd have to persuade the guys not to eat it in her presence at some point too, just looking at it on a plate made her feel a pang of sadness. But here wasn't the place. She couldn't risk upsetting her hosts. While she'd be fine if they just kicked them out of the dome, she didn't know about the others. Cam and Jared might be okay too, but Flint would certainly struggle, and she wasn't ready for that flame to be doused. At least, not until she'd had a chance to experience it, and after that, she'd probably want to keep it lit all the more.

This is your seat. The blue man gestured towards the seat that she knew was for the guest of honour, and she opened her mouth to protest before one of the men put a steadying hand on her lower back. From the temperature of his skin, her betting was on it being Cam, but she didn't turn around to be sure.

"Thank you," she acknowledged, taking her seat as gracefully as she could while wearing such a short dress. She scowled. What was it with their outfits? They were so impractical. What if there was a chill? Or she spilt dinner on herself? At least red wine wouldn't stain it. Or it would, but that'd only cover up the parts of her that were on display.

Flint took the seat to her right, while the throne to her left appeared to contain an older looking *na fir ghorma* whose hair was even more unruly than the others she'd encountered so far. Thankfully, he also seemed to be wearing more clothing, and his private parts were thankfully left to her imagination. Which reminded her...

She looked at her men, having been too conscious about what she herself was wearing to actually look at them. Unsurprisingly, they too were more covered, though the shirts they'd been given were as sheer as her dress was. Now *that* she could get on board with.

Greetings, Wardens. The man on Macey's left said. She wasn't sure how she knew that it was him speaking, but it was something almost instinctual that let her know.

"And to yourself, your Majesty," she replied sweetly, glad now that her father had enjoyed trotting her out to engage with the visiting dignitaries. It had given her a whole host of potential conversation topics as well as the ability to feign interest in anyone and anything. Though she was genuinely intrigued by who the *na fir ghorma* were exactly, and what they wanted.

My son says that you were travelling on the Staran.

"Yes," she replied, glancing quickly at Cam who was sat several places down. Hopefully, he'd come and rescue her from a conversation about something she was clueless on.

How?

Well, that wasn't what she'd expected. Then again, when she'd left the house the other day she hadn't exactly expected to be kidnapped for a reason that even escaped her kidnappers, or end up at the bottom of the sea with a bunch of blue humanoid fish people claiming to be kelpies. She snorted before catching herself. Here wasn't the place to be having uncharitable thoughts about her hosts. If they could speak into her mind, then what if they could read it too. She pushed the thought aside. There was no way that she could entertain that, otherwise they'd know what she'd been thinking about Cam and Flint doing to her later. Though maybe Flint and Cam themselves knowing wouldn't be a bad thing. Maybe they'd whisk her off from here and play out the fantasy in her head instantly.

"Cam?" she asked, not as quietly as she'd

intended. But at least it got his attention. He made his way over and placed his hands on her shoulders, giving her a strength she didn't know she needed.

"Yes, Macey?" he returned softly.

"His Majesty is asking me about the Staran." She hoped that Cam would be able to answer more. And that the King, if that's who he truly was, would ask the questions directly to him.

"How may I help?"

How do you travel the Staran?

"It's something myself and my companion have always been able to do," Cam said, gesturing to Flint as he did so. "We discovered it quite by accident I'm afraid."

That shouldn't be possible.

"I believe you're correct, and yet here we are." She felt rather than saw him shrug, and lifted one of her hands to place it gently on his, offering him the support that he may or may not need, but that she was there to give regardless.

Only our people can.

Was it her, or did the King sound slightly disbelieving? Like he didn't think they were telling the truth.

"I find that unlikely, your majesty. There are too many races in the world for you to be the only ones who can travel the Staran, even if you didn't have proof that's not the case standing right in front of you. I can assure you that myself and Flint are perfectly capable of travelling through them, and bringing other people with us if we so choose. That's how Jared and Macey got here, in case you're wondering." Cam didn't sound happy at all, and Macey longed to do more to back him up, but didn't know how without making matters worse. After all, she knew even less than the King did about the Staran.

The King's eyes were even more bulging now and his big mouth was opening and closing rapidly. He was not impressed, not at all.

The Staran were made for us.

That peaked her interest. "Who made it for you?"

The Sìth. We made a bargain with them and in return we got the Staran. We are a people of the sea, yet we need to travel to other places occasionally, faster than we could swim. It's our lifeline, and now it's malfunctioning. Are you sure this is not your fault?

The accusation was clear to see in his face. Macey was glad it wasn't directed at her - but at the same time, she was angry at her mens' behalf.

"How long ago did they build it for you?" she asked, having a slight suspicion. If what she'd heard about the Sìth was correct, this might be a slight disaster. They were the Scottish fae, kin to the Sidhe in Ireland. And mostly, they were trouble.

Seventy years ago when my grandfather struck the deal with them.

Cam sighed, having come to the same conclusion as Macey.

"I've been travelling the Staran for centuries. They didn't build them for you. All they did was give you access to it. You've been tricked, your Majesty."

The King rose to his feet, roaring his displeasure. For a species not using their mouths to talk, he certainly had a very loud voice. Their vocal chords seemed to be intact.

Cam squeezed Macey's hand reassuringly and she frowned. Did he think she was scared of the merman? She'd met a lot of scarier creatures, that was for sure. One of them being her Aunt Nessie.

The thing with scary people is that once she got to know them, she could see behind the façade. Most of them were more scared of themselves than scared of her. All they do is project their own fear to the outside world.

Father, calm yourself. You're scaring our guests.

Muahwa, the crown prince, put a hand on his father's shoulder and gently made him sit down again. The silence that had fallen quickly became a buzzing noise again as people resumed their conversations and feasting.

That reminded Macey that she hadn't even started to eat. With all that Staran conversation, she hadn't even noticed how one of the servants had put a covered plate in front of her. Well, not a real plate.

It was a massive, white scallop containing... algae soup? Perhaps? It was hard to tell from the green slime staring back at her. It looked very alive. And disgusting.

There were several ways of preparing algae, and this was not one of them. She took her fork and aimlessly stirred the green mass. It squelched.

This feast was going to be one big disappointment.

Are your rooms to your liking? Muahwa asked, having taken a seat on his father's side.

Macey blushed at the thought of what she'd done there not long ago, but court etiquette had schooled her not to show embarrassment. Instead, she nodded curtly.

"Thank you very much for your hospitality. I'm assuming we'll talk about the reason why we're here after the feast?"

Yes, we will. Do you not like our sea snail algae mousse?

Her stomach did a flip. Now she was glad she hadn't touched the food yet. Sea snail! What barbarians!

She cleared her throat. "I'm a vegetarian."

That was as good an excuse as any.

What is that?

Okay, maybe not such a good excuse.

It was strange how both kelpies and *na fir ghorma* both lived underwater, but had such different lifestyles. Maybe living in a loch surrounded by human civilisation had made her more aware of the outside world than these people stuck on the bottom of the ocean.

"I don't eat meat," she explained and the crown prince looked at her in wonder.

But what else non-meat is there but algae?

"Kelp, water lilies, water chestnuts, reedmace and many others. There's a wide variety of plants in lakes, if you look closely. Most of us don't eat the other creatures we share the lochs with. Don't you have fish as pets?"

Muahwa laughed. *We don't live in the water. How should we have fish in here?* He pointed at the hall, completely dry and filled with air.

Macey felt like an idiot. Of course, they didn't have fish living with them. Which probably explained why they ate them - just like the King, who was currently munching on the fried fin of a seabass.

11

ome, Muahwa said after the meal had finished. Macey sighed. She was hungry, grumpy and really didn't want to have to deal with whatever it was Muahwa wanted. Regardless, she stood up to follow him, dimly aware of the three men doing the same. Good. That meant she wouldn't have to face whatever this was alone. There was a certain kind of comfort in that.

No one said anything as they were taken into a small, but comfortable looking room. Like everywhere else, the roof was entirely see-through, allowing a rare glimpse into a world no one else could see. Unlike everywhere else, the wall to the outside was also unencumbered, and Macey drifted over towards it, entranced by the underwater world.

She'd never felt as small and unworldly as she did

at that moment, looking into the great abyss before her, with the creatures she'd never swum with going about their lives. The bottom of the sea held wonders and dangers that she couldn't even imagine, and hadn't had a reason to until now. In fact, the home of the *na fir ghorma* only proved it more to her. She hadn't even realised the other kelpies existed, so what else did the sea hold? Other than mermaids and selkies, she had no real clue. And she wasn't in any rush to meet any of them given her Aunt Nessie's stories about them.

Beautiful, isn't it? Muahwa asked, stepping up beside her to look out into the ocean. A large shadow passed overhead at that moment, and Macey looked up in awe as what looked like a basking shark swum over head. The huge, but surprisingly graceful and gentle creature was something to behold. She couldn't even work out whether she wanted to swim with it or not. It'd be an experience that was for sure. But at the same time, the sea was a lot bigger than the loch she'd grown up in.

"Yes," she whispered.

It's in trouble. He sounded resigned, and she once again marvelled at the emotions he could convey just by speaking in her head. Or maybe he could convey more *because* he was speaking in her head. She was just going to go with it. After the events of the past few days, that was really her only option. Especially if she wanted to stay sane

"In trouble from what?" she asked, conscious of the silence in the room which meant her men were likely listening intently too. Though given that Muahwa could speak directly into their heads anyway, it wouldn't matter if there was an entire brass band playing the loudest fanfare they could muster, they'd still be able to hear.

The Sìth.

"But you father sai—"

My father is a fool. He thinks that the world revolves around the na fir ghorma, that we're far more than the tiny drop in the ocean than we are.

Macey chewed on her bottom lip, not quite sure how she was meant to respond to that. She hadn't been particularly expecting a Prince to speak so blatantly against his father.

"What are the Sìth doing?" She wasn't sure she really wanted to know, but needed to nonetheless. Especially if she *was* a Warden.

We're not entirely sure. She wondered briefly who 'we' were, but now wasn't the time to ask. Hopefully, it would come clear in time.

"Helpful," Jared muttered behind her, and she just about managed to stop herself from throwing him a glare. Comments like that really weren't helpful.

"What do you think they're up to then?" she

asked instead, hoping Muahwa would ignore Jared. She made a mental note to punish him for it later. Maybe she'd find out what his deepest fantasy was and then do it in front of him with Flint or Cam. Or Flint and Cam. Oops. Probably best not to have thoughts like that while discussing something as serious as she was.

We need you to find out.

"Wait, what? I thought you wanted us here so you could explain the problem to us?" She felt a little outraged. This was a complete waste of time if it wasn't actually going to help them get any further forward.

Did you know there was a problem before coming here?

"No," Macey said.

"Yes," Flint countered, stepping forward and pressing his hand into the small of Macey's back. "We couldn't get to Earth," he reminded her, his eyes softening with affection as he looked at her. She could get used to that. Very much so.

And you weren't doing anything about it? Muahwa's face didn't change, but his inflexion brought raised eyebrows to mind.

"We'd only just discovered the issue," Flint countered. "We were on our way to do something about it." Macey placed a calming hand on his arm, hoping that he wouldn't go any further. She could tell just from the way he was speaking that he was on the verge of getting defensive. And while she kind of liked his riled-up side, here really wasn't the place. Flames were easily doused by water, and that was all around them.

Ah.

"We were on our way to visit Malan before you interrupted us," Macey said softly, using all her diplomatic skills to try and ensure that this didn't end badly. How had she ended up with someone so hot-headed? She smothered a snort. Hot-headed. She wondered exactly how far that would go...

Malan won't have the answers.

"Do you know that for sure?" Cam asked. "Malan is a prophet." He sounded so reasonable, particularly compared to the other two.

No, but Malan's powers are limited, I doubt he will know any more than I do.

Macey crossed her arms and turned to face the Prince. "So what you're saying is that something, somewhere is wrong. You think it's the Sith doing it, but no one knows anything that might help us."

Pretty much. He sounded amused. Least that made one of them.

"And why aren't you doing something about this yourself?" Macey asked, annoyed at the expectations he seemed to have. Just because that Malan guy had come up with a prophecy didn't mean that she'd actually have to believe in it. And even if it was true, nowhere did it say that the Wardens had to help the *na fir ghorma* deal with the Sìth. Couldn't they just fight it out among themselves? Macey had more important things to do, and most of them involved the three men standing behind her. Waves, they promised her a waffle!

We cannot leave the sea for long. We are bound to the water and wither away the further we are away from it. The Staran are a grey zone in which we can stay longer than on land, but now that it is no longer working as it used to, we are stranded here in our underwater home.

Muahwa actually looked quite sad, if his expression could be interpreted as such. The giant mouth made it hard to guess what he was feeling.

Maybe the *na fir ghorma* weren't that similar to the kelpies after all. Not many kelpies wanted to leave their lochs, but it didn't do them any harm if they did. Most didn't like their human looks though, so they preferred to be half or fully shifted in the water.

Thinking of shifting made Macey's skin itch. She was surrounded by water yet she wasn't able to swim in it. Maybe she could persuade them to give her some alone time later on. The seawater was calling to her and after the terrible chlorinated pool water in the guys' home, this would be pure bliss.

"So what do you want us to do?" she asked, still not sure about the blue man's intentions.

Travel to the Sìth. Talk to them. If they control the

Staran and they're no longer working as they should, it must be their doing. Force them to return things to how they were before. Maybe that will calm the storms.

"Wait, how are the Staran linked to the weather?" This was getting more confusing by the minute.

This time it was Cam who answered. "The Staran link the worlds. Imagine it as the glue that keeps them connected. That they allow us to travel on it is just a side effect, I believe. I don't think that the Sith created them, either. It's sentient somehow, and much more powerful than they are. No, if the Staran are not allowing us to travel on it, it's a symptom that something is seriously wrong with them."

"Could it be... ill?" Macey asked, still getting used to thinking of this bridge between worlds as sentient.

"Not sure that is the right term, but yes. I think something bad is happening to it." Cam shot Muahwa an annoyed glance. "And I still think that Malan will be able to help us."

Go to him if you wish, but I believe you are wasting your time. If you manage to get to him in the first place.

That was true of course. If it hadn't let them travel to Earth earlier... wait a moment.

"We're on Earth now, right?" she asked, the wheels in her head turning.

Yes. We're on the Earthen Plane.

She ignored the weird way Muahwa described her home and turned to the guys.

"Flint, you said the Staran didn't let us travel to Earth, but they did. Just not to the destination you had in mind. So it's not completely broken. Maybe it knew we were needed here. Maybe it wanted us to meet the *na fir ghorma*. If it's sentient, then it knows something that we don't. Maybe it's trying to send us a message. Maybe it wants us to investigate the Sìth just like Muahwa says."

"Or maybe it just wanted us to see how other races are affected," Cam pondered. "I bet that when we next travel on the Staran, they will bring us to where we need to be and not where we want to go."

"Goodbye waffles," Jared sighed and inside, Macey did the same. The food at the feast had not been satisfactory in the least. She could do with some sugary, fatty goodness. Like waffles. Or something fried. The Scots loved to fry their food, even sweets. Deep-fried Mars bars... heavenly.

But she was itching to find out if Cam's theory was correct. Not knowing where you'd end up was exciting, in a way. Also a little scary, but as long as she wasn't travelling alone it should be fine. If she'd had her powers, it would be different, but without them, she was as helpless as a human.

"Maybe we could stop at my father's palace to get my powers unlocked?" she said to nobody in particular.

I think I can help with that.

She looked at Muahwa in surprise. So far, she hadn't seen any of the na fir ghorma display magical abilities. With the exception of them talking in their heads, if that counted as magic.

He laughed at her surprised expression.

Not me personally, but our fearsaidh, our tribe's wise man. He will know what to do.

"Then let's go to him. I want to leave as soon as possible." Macey noticed how impolite that sounded. "To find help for you, of course. Your hospitality has been much appreciated."

THE FEARSAIDH WAS the ugliest storm kelpie she'd seen to date. His scales looked grey and brittle as if they'd fall off any second. Half of his teeth were missing and the others were yellowed with age. His eyes were milky white and Macey assumed that he was blind.

Welcome, daughter of the lake. Welcome, men of the wind, fire and earth.

"Pleased to meet you," Macey replied, proud of her diplomatic training. She didn't think her expression gave away the slight disgust she felt for the old man's appearance. "Muahwa says you can help me with my magic? My father locked it but I have need of it now." She skipped the small talk this time. She'd had enough of that. All she wanted was her powers back so that they could leave this strange place and people. She loved being underwater, but she preferred to actually be *in* the water. This weird in-between state was giving her the creeps.

Your father had good reason to lock them. For some reason, you are stronger on earth than you are on the water. You could have unknowingly destroyed yourself and others, had you tried to use it. But now things have changed. You are no longer alone. You are part of the Seven, and with each Warden you bind to, your powers will become more controlled. Stronger, too.

"Wait a second. I need to bind to the other Wardens to get my powers back? What does that mean?"

You should know. You're already bound to one.

Waves. The strange tattoo. Did she unknowingly bind herself to Jared? To an incubus?

Fuck.

Malan, the Prophet

12

She couldn't believe she was about to go through the Staran again. To feel the nothingness. But this was the only way they had to get to Malan apparently. She felt the waves singing in her blood, a sure sign that the fearsaidh was right, her magic had already started unlocking. All she needed to do to finish unlocking it was to bind with the other Wardens. Well, that wasn't happening. Not if her life depended on it. But even so, she was pleased that she knew it was possible to get access to her powers again. It made her feel a lot more in control of herself.

"I still say we should stop off and get some waffles," Jared murmured under his breath. Macey threw him a dirty look over her shoulder. And not the kind of dirty look he'd want either. No. He lost

148

the right to any of those the moment he claimed her and made a fucking tattoo appear on her back. Sure, he claimed he had no idea how it happened, but somehow, she didn't believe him. Or didn't *want* to believe him. If she did, she'd likely have to accept the stupid Warden thing too. And she wasn't prepared to do that yet. Not until she'd heard it from Flint's prophet.

"We don't have time to stop for waffles," Cam reasoned. She was surprised by how calm he sounded, and not at all like they were responsible for some serious saving. Actually, she kind of liked how assured he was. There was no doubt he'd do what needed to be done. There was something about the voice that heated her up in places she really shouldn't be thinking about right now.

"Maybe Malan will have some," Jared added. Macey rolled her eyes, thankful that none of them could see her from where they were stood behind.

"I doubt ghostly prophets stock the kitchen," Flint said, amusement lingering just below the surface. Macey didn't turn to look at him. If she did, she'd probably see the smirk that was surely on Jared's face, and then she'd melt. And forget to be mad at him. Come to think of it, she was kind of melting a little already. Damn incubus.

"How would you know? Are you a ghostly prophet? He loves waffles."

"I find it highly unlikely that he makes them himself." Flint's voice cracked, and Macey almost stifled the giggle she'd been suppressing.

"Ah, so you're not too mad at me then, little kelpie." Her giggle ended, and something very different to amusement flooded through her. Especially as Jared's voice sounded closer than it had before. A *lot* closer.

Strong arms circled her, and without meaning to, she leaned back into him, enjoying the closeness.

"No, I suppose not," she grumbled.

"I really didn't know what was happening, I swear it." She twisted her head to the left so that she was looking at him, and noticed the overwhelming earnestness in his eyes.

"I know," she half-whispered. His expression changed before her eyes as a large grin spread across his face. He leaned in and kissed her quickly, not lingering for a second. Much to her disappointment.

"I'm glad."

"Right, now that's sorted. Shall we?" Flint asked, waving his hand towards the Staran in front of them. Macey nodded, untangling herself from Jared's arms, and making her way towards him. She wrapped her arms around Flint's waist, wishing it was her legs instead. Looking up at him, she saw the soft smile on his lips. He was clearly feeling a lot better than while they'd been under water. For that she was glad.

"Ready when you are," she said.

"Oh, I'm always ready for you." He wiggled his eyebrows at her, and Macey's skin flushed just thinking of all the things he would do. She decided she needed some alone time with him soon.

"Let's get going, Flame-Man."

"I see you've finally arrived," an echoey voice greeted them as Macey's feet touched the ground, and she pulled away from Flint. While weird, at least this voice wasn't just in her head. She'd had enough of those kinds of voices after the encounter in her bedroom and with the storm kelpies.

She turned in the direction of the voice, before stumbling back slightly in shock, narrowly avoiding falling only through the steadying hand Flint placed on her elbow. A head floated in front of them. An honest-to-the-seas head. It was a little bigger than a normal head, maybe about the size of Macey's chest, with a long flowing beard and hair. Oh and had she mentioned the lack of body? Or the fact that it was white and ever so slightly translucent?

"Malan," Cam acknowledged, taking a step forward.

"Camdan, good to see you again."

"Again?" Cam frowned, and Macey wanted to take

a step towards him and offer support. But that meant going closer to the head. No, Malan, she shouldn't keep thinking about him as just a head. That would be rude when she knew his name.

"For me, yes. I watch all of the new Wardens. Macey, Flint, Jared," he acknowledged them one by one with a nod. Which was impressive in the circumstances.

"New?" Macey squeaked.

"Well, yes. You didn't think you were the first Wardens, did you?"

"I'm not even sure I'm any Warden," she muttered.

"Oh, you are, little Kelpie Princess. But you're not the first. Nor even the second. Nor will you be the last. Though I suspect you may last longer than the previous ones. Humans can be so fragile, even when blessed with eternal life." Malan sighed wistfully, as if it was of no great importance that he'd just announced other Wardens had died.

Macey wanted to take a step back, to get as far away from the prophet as possible. But something was telling her that she needed to hear this. That, actually, even if she didn't want to accept it, this was her fate, and she'd probably better get used to it.

"I'm not human," Macey said defiantly, refusing to let the head-prophet see how insecure she felt in his presence. "I'm kelpie."

"Yes, you are. The Fates have decided to mix it up a bit. Good. It was getting boring."

She stared at him, unable to hide her disbelief. How could he be so nonchalant? He was talking about other Wardens dying, for waves' sake.

Malan sighed. "If you'd seen as many people pass through my doors only to die a few decades later as I have, you'd be the same, little kelpie. Now ask your questions, chop chop. And no, Jared, I don't have waffles."

The big question Macey wanted to ask was 'what happened to the rest of your body', but she'd been raised to be more polite than that.

"What exactly are Wardens?" Macey asked and Malan's stern glance turned to the guys.

"You've not told her?"

"Ehm, we don't know a lot ourselves," Jared defended himself.

"There are seven of you, one for each element. Some generations of Wardens don't have to do much except existing to keep the balance. But sometimes, like in your case, you have to come together to heal the worlds. So no pressure." He grinned. "Next question."

"Who is hurting the Staran?" Cam asked and Malan sighed again.

"Wrong question. Next."

Cam looked confused. "Why are they hurting them?"

"Wrong."

Macey grimaced. "Are the Staran actually being hurt?"

"Clever girl." Malan's head bobbed around in approval, giving her a slight sense of vertigo. She still wanted to find out why he only had a head. Even ghosts deserved a full body.

He didn't seem to be in the mood to expand, so she frowned, trying to figure out what he was not telling them. "If the Staran are not being hurt and are deteriorating nonetheless, they must either be ill or hurting themselves." She paused. "I'm talking about it like it's a living thing... is that correct?"

Malan did something that looked like a smile. "They're not hurting themselves."

"Then they're ill. What is making them ill?" She was starting to feel a little silly now. Was she going to ask next whether the mist was suffering from the flu? Maybe a chest infection? Waves, this was weird.

"I can't tell you that."

"Because you don't want to?" Cam barged in, more annoyance lacing his voice than Macey would have liked.

"Because I do not know. I can tell you what's wrong with them, but not what is causing it. That is the Wardens' task to find out."

"And how the hell are we supposed to do that?" Macey put her hand on Cam's arm, trying to calm him down a little. Not that she wasn't asking the same questions in her head. Just... his anger was making Malan's head more translucent. She had a feeling that he could disappear whenever he wanted. And they needed answers before he did that.

"First, you need to find the other Wardens. You are only strong when you're all together. Seven elements, seven Wardens, seven problems. The Staran are strong, they couldn't be hurt by just one thing. It's a multitude of factors coming together and combined they are stronger than they would be on their own. There is not much time left. Soon, nobody will be able to travel on the Staran, and the worlds will drift apart. We can't let that happen."

"We? I thought it was us who had to do all the work?" Jared quipped, a smirk on his lips. Much better than Cam's anger, Macey decided. She was going to reward him with a kiss later on.

"I won't be coming with you, little incubus. I'm bound to this place, but I will be able to monitor you from afar. The Mahoun isn't the only one who's got eyes and ears everywhere. And just because I don't enter your pretty head, doesn't mean that I can't."

"The Mahoun? Entering my head? What?" Macey was confused.

"It's what he calls himself. The devil. Don't think

that's what he is, but his past and future are shrouded in mist. All I can see is the present, and he is preparing. He wants the Staran to fail. He knows the Wardens will be the only ones who can thwart him, so he's hunting you, even now. One of you is already in his clutches, and another one will be soon."

"Oh, you mean the Voice?" Macey exclaimed, her head hurting at the memory. It all started to make sense now. Well, a little bit, at least.

Malan chuckled. "He wouldn't like that name. He's used to be called the Terrifying, the Monster, the Devil, not the Voice. Bit boring, if you ask me."

Macey grimaced. "He hurt me."

Malan turned serious. "He did. And he will do it again. He's doing it to one of the Seven just now. But before you can go find the others, you four need to bond. You need to be strong together or you will be torn apart. You need your magic, Macey, or you won't have a chance. And you know how to unlock it."

He actually winked. Macey shuddered a little. That was creepy. He knew that she was going to have to have sex with the remaining two guys. And while she didn't have a problem with the actual act - waves, she was feeling the arousal coming even at this moment - but this weird ghost head knowing... yuck. Who knew how detailed his visions were. Did that make him a pervert?

Flint noticed her unease and put an arm around

her shoulders. She leaned against him, savouring the warmth of his body.

"Where shall we go now? If we can't find the others yet and don't know how to heal the Staran, what is our task?"

Besides having sex, Macey added in her mind. She didn't think that was the only thing they could do. That was tempting, but quite unproductive.

"You must visit the Sìth. The *na fìr ghorma* are right about them being connected to the Staran, but not how they think. They have been the Staran's guardians for millennia, but they are having trouble keeping it working. They can use your help... or maybe you can use theirs."

13

She almost couldn't believe they were back at the house. This wasn't getting them anywhere. It certainly wasn't helping find her brothers, or clearing their names, or doing whatever it was that Wardens were supposed to do. Surely they should be getting on with that?

Oh damn. Guessed that meant she'd finally accepted that she was a Warden. Bye, bye plausible deniability.

She glanced at the three men, who were looking slightly nervous and uncomfortable. Probably because they'd also been told that they had to perform on demand. She just hoped they felt like her and *wanted* to have sex, but were just a little on edge for having to have it. Huh, maybe this was how Jared felt most of the time. A wave of affection, and concern flooded through Macey. The poor man. Least he had her now, she could keep up with what he needed. Possibly. If Malan was to be believed, then she had a lot of keeping up with needs to do in her future.

So long as her own were met.

"Oh, this is ridiculous," she said, grabbing the hem of her shirt and whipping it over her head as three pairs of eyes zoned in on her. Good, that was more like it.

"Okay, I'll be in my room if you need me," Jared said, clearing his throat loudly. Before making his way to the door.

"Wait, you're not..." Macey trailed off, trying to plead with him using her eyes as he turned to face her. Jared changed his trajectory, swiftly closing the distance between them and caressing her cheek tenderly.

"Not this time, no. If I stay, then I'll want you all to myself. And if my incubus takes over...well, then you'll never get the bonds with the others sealed." He leaned forward and pressed a sweet kiss to her lips. She longed to deepen it and make it go further but had to respect his wishes. She couldn't push further than he was willing to go, and still expect the opposite to be true. Then again, him pushing had been highly enjoyable.

"Next time?" she asked, a small whimper slipping out at the end of her question.

"Definitely," he said the word softly, then pressed his forehead against hers in a gesture that was surprisingly intimate. "Have fun, little kelpie." His face took on a wicked look as warm hands smoothed over the skin of Macey's back. Flint was behind her then.

She shuddered, leaning back into him as Jared pulled away. She watched him leave but was soon distracted by the small kisses Flint was trailing along the side of her neck, and the hand that was pressing on her stomach and pulling her towards him more.

"Didn't anyone tell you it's good practice to share?" Cam's eyes twinkled as he asked, and Flint chuckled against her neck, the vibrations travelling down her body and desperately making her want to slip her hand down her jeans and relieve the tension she was already feeling.

The tension that was completely natural, it had to be without Jared's influence anywhere near. And she assumed that he didn't need feeding either, otherwise he'd have stayed to watch at the very least. Or maybe he could feed from a distance? She'd have to ask him about that later.

All thoughts fled her mind as Cam pressed his body against her front, capturing her lips with his and kissing her with a passion she hadn't quite expected.

He'd been the gentlest of the three of them so far, but this was something far more primal about this kiss. Especially as it was pressing her back into Flint, whose hardness rubbed against her ass.

She pushed at the hem of Cam's shirt, desperate for him to take it off, but whimpering when his hands and lips left her while he did so.

"I'm not going anywhere," Cam said, pulling down her lower lip, making her bite it involuntarily. He groaned. "You're going to be my undoing." His voice was low and husky, sending shivers through her.

Or that might have been Flint's hand creeping across her stomach and unbuttoning her jeans so he could slip a hand down them. He slipped his fingers as far as they could go, but, much to her disappointment, he was restricted by the tight denim.

"Do you trust me?" he whispered against the shell of her ear, before taking it between his teeth and giving it a nip. If the two of them carried on, she wasn't going to last until the main event.

"Yes," she moaned as Cam pressed kisses across her collarbone. She threaded her hands through his hair and tugged on it, desperate for him not to let up.

"Remember that," Flint said, pulling back a little and placing his hands on either of her thighs. She was just thankful that his hard, hot chest was still pressed against her back, even if he was annoyingly clothed still.

Her legs began to prickle, heating a surprising amount. But it felt good, almost as if whatever Flint was doing was adding to the pleasure building inside her. Though that was unlikely. It was probably just that she was already on edge from the attentions of the two of them. And still on a high after sleeping with Jared.

A cool breeze fluttered against her legs. That must have been Cam's doing. She tried to look down, but that was the moment Cam chose to rip her bra away from her, and twist her nipple between his fingers. She moaned, tipping her head back and resting it against Flint's chest. He chuckled, slipping his hand around her body and palming her other breast.

His other hand was resting on her naked hip. Wait...naked? Hadn't she been wearing jeans just a moment before? Oh no...if he'd burned her clothes off, he was going to have a whole shit storm coming...

Her thoughts disappeared as Flint's hand slipped between her legs, teasing in a sinfully delicious way. If he kept doing that, he could burn anything off that he wanted. As many times as he wanted.

She knew that she was playing with fire, but luckily, she was water. She was going to extinguish whatever they threw at her. With every kiss that the men left on her skin, she could feel the barriers around her magic break down. If only she had known this before.

She'd have taken them into her bed much earlier. It was the best excuse ever.

Flint began to fuck her hard with his fingers and she moaned, pressing her thighs together to prevent herself from climaxing too soon. All that held her upright was being sandwiched between Flint and Cam's chests. Cam was massaging her breasts, playing with her nipples in a way that made her lightheaded the more she concentrated on the sensation. Wasn't Jared supposed to be the sex demon? She'd never heard of wraiths being known for their pleasuring skills... but here they were, making her feel better than she ever had before.

When her moans became erratic, Flint gently lowered her onto the floor, where Cam was already waiting. How did she not notice him leaving her? He was lying on his back, fully erect, ready to sink into her folds. Well, she was just as ready. Too much so, in fact, she was having a hard time not coming immediately. Flint had a way with moving his fingers that left her breathless and trembling. He helped her sit down on Cam's cock and she moaned as she felt him fill her to the brink. He was large; she was glad Flint had prepared her so well. When she had taken him fully inside, she breathed a sigh of relief, which quickly turned into a groan when Cam began to slowly move in her. He gripped her hips and directed her movements until she was swaying her hips in a circle. It felt incredible.

Flint was standing nearby, touching himself as he watched them. Macey smiled and licked her lips, motioning him towards her. She grabbed his cock and kissed his tip long and gently, then wrapped her lips around him.

"Macey, this is not a good idea," Flint groaned as she began to run her tongue up and down his length. She looked up at him and fluttered her eyelashes in what she hoped was a seductive gaze. He arched his back as she sucked hard, making him twitch in her mouth.

"Don't forget me," Cam whispered and she noticed that her movements had slowed. Cam was doing all the work, pressing his hips upwards to reach new depths. Macey grinned - which was hard given that she still had Flint's cock in her mouth - and began to move up and down, almost to the point where Cam slipped out of her. But never that far. She wasn't experienced but somehow, she knew what she was doing. And the guys seemed to enjoy it. More than enjoy it, judging from their ragged breaths and groans.

She was running out of air and had to stop for a moment, taking Flint out of her mouth. He used the pause to step behind her, going on his knees.

"Do you trust me?" he asked again, and she

nodded, breathless. What was he planning to do this time? There was nothing left to burn.

Then she felt a finger at her back entrance, that dark, forbidden place that nobody had ever touched before. Flint gently rubbed the sensitive skin around her ass and she leaned forwards until she was fully lying on Cam's chest. Her nipples rubbed against his hard muscles as she moved, somehow trying to both escape and get closer to Flint's teasing finger.

The pressure increased until he entered her slowly. He was gentle and careful, but it was sore nonetheless. Macey was tempted to ask him to stop, but then his other hand began to play with the most sensitive spot between her legs and all protest was forgotten. By the time he added a second finger, she was a quivering mess, squirming on Cam's chest. The wind Warden was whispering calming words to her but only half of them reached her brain. She was in another sphere, a place filled with nothing but pleasure, a place she shared with the two men.

It didn't surprise her when Flint replaced his fingers with his hard cock. She was stretched to the max but then Flint began to move in her, rubbing against the thin skin separating him from Cam, and she screamed, the most intense climax she'd ever experienced ripping through her. She vaguely noticed some exploding sounds in the distance but all she cared about was the trembles and shivers racking her body, the kisses pressed on her skin, the whispered words from her men. Their movements became faster, more forceful, until they came to their own peak, roaring their achievement through the room.

Exhausted, Macey let herself rest on Cam's warm chest, not even protesting as Flint slipped out of her and left the room. She wrapped her legs around Cam's, hugging him tight as tiredness swept over her. She was so happy. It wouldn't have surprised her if the whole world had changed in the past hour. And something else was new.

She could feel a trickle of energy pouring into her. The walls her father had put around her magic were collapsing. It wasn't long now until they'd be gone completely. Her magic was finally returning.

A warm, wet towel suddenly appeared between her legs, cleaning her. Flint had returned.

"I need to deal with some exploded pipes in a moment, but I wanted to make sure you're alright first," he whispered, leaving a trail of kisses on her back.

"Why wouldn't I be?" she asked in confusion, her voice quiet from exhaustion.

"You made several pipes burst and I believe our basement is flooded."

Cam chuckled, his chest vibrating against Macey's body. It made her love him even more.

Wait, love?

Was that what she felt?

"Looks like our kelpie has her powers back," Cam observed, gently stroking Macey's hair.

She was confused. She'd not intended for anything to explode. Maybe that's why she was so exhausted. She'd not used magic in almost three years.

14

Sleep sounded like a good idea. A *really* good idea. At least if anyone had asked Macey, that's what she'd have said. Except that her men seemed to have other plans.

She sighed deeply, partly from the satisfaction that was flowing through her still, and partly from the fact they were being so damn stubborn.

"How're you feeling?" Jared asked, twining his arms around her waist and pulling her back to him. She relaxed into his arms, enjoying the soothing feel of him next to her.

"Good. A little tired."

He chuckled. "I'm not surprised, little kelpie. You made quite the mess."

She blushed, thinking of the burst pipes and flooded basement Flint had dealt with. Maybe it wasn't the best idea to let her fire wraith go fix a problem very much caused by her water powers, but then, it had needed sorting, and it wasn't like she'd been in the position to do anything. She hadn't been in the position to do much but laze around, boneless and sated.

"Remind me why I can't spend the day in bed?" she whined, making Jared chuckle more.

"What makes you think you'd get any rest there?"

Macey's blood heated, and a wave of desire crashed through her, despite the fact she hadn't long slept with two of her men. She shouldn't be ready for more again, not when she was still sore and aching, but in the best possible way.

"Well, I…"

"We'd let you rest, but there are far more important things we need to do."

She frowned. It was true, she just didn't want to accept that. "Lightning?" She sighed. She didn't even know the person and she was already part of a plan to save them.

"Yes, we need to save her," Jared answered instantly.

"Her…" Macey repeated, turning the idea around in her head. She didn't like the idea of another woman around, not when she'd just managed to capture the three of their attentions.

"Apparently." Jared sounded confused, as if he wasn't too sure what he was saying either.

"You don't know?"

"Not for sure, but it felt like the right thing to say."

She felt his shrug against her back.

"Probably true then." She tried to squash down the jealousy that was clawing about inside her.

"There's no need to be jealous, little kelpie," he whispered in her ear. She shivered. Everything he did just made her think of sex, and this was no different. The only thing she wasn't sure of, was whether it was because of his incubus side, or just because of who he was to her.

"How did you..."

"I'm an incubus. Attraction and sex aren't the only things I can sense. I'm sensitive to a lot of emotions. And jealousy is so tightly tied to what I'm strongest in, that it's one I can sense clearly."

"Oh."

"But don't worry, Macey." His lips actually brushed over her ear this time, and she shivered in anticipation. "You're already ours and we're already yours. You're already wearing our marks after all." He traced his hand gently over her back, about where the tattoo she'd gained after having sex with him was.

"I've got two more, don't I?" she asked carefully, not at all surprised.

"Without a doubt."

"What do they look like?" She was breathing heavily, just the idea of bearing their marks enough to get her heart racing and her body heating up. She was going to die from orgasm overload if they carried on.

"I don't know for sure without looking, but remove your shirt and I'll tell you," he teased. She wasn't all that sure how serious he was being, but pulled away from him and turned so they were facing one another. Slowly, she raised the hem of her shirt, Jared's hungry eyes following every inch of exposed skin. She grinned to herself, pleased with the effect she was no doubt having. "You're beautiful," he said reverently, and her heart swelled to three times the size. Fitting given she had three times the normal number of men in her life.

"Thanks." She dropped her shirt to the floor and gave him a hooded look, knowing full well what it would do to him. Though really, he was probably already there given she was standing before him in a lacy black bra and jeans that made her ass look fabulous.

"Turn around," he commanded, twirling his finger. She complied, heat washing over her as she pictured the last time he'd been this way.

His finger came to rest on her skin, and he began to trace a pattern, leaving a trail of goosebumps in his path.

"This one is my mark." He traced it again. "It's the symbol for earth."

"You like that you were first, don't you?" she asked, her words hitching at the end. There was no way she could deny what he did to her then.

"Very much so." His finger trailed across her skin, stopping when he reached the opposite shoulder where he traced a different pattern. "This one is for wind. It's Cam's mark."

"Why is it in that place?" she asked, trying to keep her mind focused on what they were talking about and not the sensations of his touch.

"I think it's because we're opposites. So our marks have appeared opposite one another."

"Oh. But doesn't that mean that Flint and I..."

"Yes, your marks should be opposite one another too, unless..."

"Unless?"

"Don't mind me, Macey. You don't have a water mark yet. But here's Flint's." His fingers lowered slightly, still in line with where Cam's mark was. He traced the pattern slowly, and surely, and she could picture it in her mind.

"Why don't I have a mark for me yet?" It didn't make any sense. If she was water, then surely she should've started with that one? And it felt uneven to have two marks on one side and only a single one of the other. What was with that? And what did she need to do to make her own mark appear? Having sex with herself obviously didn't do the trick, or it would have arrived already.

"I don't know. I have a theory, but I don't think you're ready to hear it just yet."

"Jared..." she drew out his name like a plea.

"Not yet, Macey. Not yet."

"Come on, tell—"

A burning pain rammed into Macey's skull and she screamed as she felt her body fall backwards at the same time as her mind was ripped away.

"HAVE YOU MISSED ME?"

The Voice was back, and it seemed even stronger this time. So much pain. Macey was struggling to hold onto sanity as agony threatened to overwhelm her. It would be so easy to give in, to be swept away...

"I WAS WRONG."

Even in her haze, she knew that it was strange for the villain to admit that he'd been wrong. "Huh?" was all she managed to say.

"YOU AREN'T THE SECOND. YOU WILL BE MY THIRD. ICE IS WALKING STRAIGHT INTO MY TRAP, THINKING HE CAN RESCUE HIS PARTNER. WHAT A FOOL. TOMORROW, I'LL HAVE LIGHTNING AND ICE, AND WATER WILL BE MY THIRD. I AM CLOSE

NOW, LITTLE KELPIE. DON'T STRUGGLE, YOU KNOW YOU CAN'T WIN."

That made sense. He was strong, powerful, she was just a girl. She couldn't fight him. It was pointless. Maybe she should just give in. Let him take her.

"GOOD GIRL. TELL ME THAT YOU WANT ME TO TAKE YOU AWAY. JUST SAY THOSE WORDS."

Yes, that sounded easy. If only she could speak. She was too weak to form words, too weak to even form proper thoughts. But him taking her sounded good. Painless. Maybe he'd take the pain away.

"YES, EVERYTHING WILL BE ALRIGHT ONCE YOU'RE WITH ME. YOU WON'T FEEL ANY PAIN. YOU'LL BE HAPPY."

Happy. But wasn't she happy already? She was having a hard time remembering why that was. Something about other people. Her men. The memories came flooding in and the Voice screamed as Macey's magic fizzled into life.

"I'LL BE BACK. NEXT TIME YOU'LL BE WEAK ENOUGH FOR ME TO BREAK THROUGH. SAY GOODBYE TO YOUR WARDENS WHILE YOU CAN. I ONLY NEED FOUR OF YOU, SO NOT ALL OF THEM WILL BE NECESSARY."

With a final hit against her mental barriers, he

disappeared and Macey was flung back into her body. Which was not a good thing.

It hurt so bad. Everything was burning. She needed water, quickly. Lots of it. She could feel her kelpie form pressuring her to be let out. Shifting would make the pain go away, but for that she needed water. Kelpies couldn't breathe on land and could only hold their breath for so long.

"Water," she whispered, not knowing if anyone was listening. She was too feeble to even open her eyes. The pain was still as bad as when the Voice had been inside her, if not worse. She gave her magic free reign and sighed in relief as cool water touched her skin. It made the pain slightly more bearable.

Someone picked her up and carried her. There were voices, noises, doors banging, but all she could do was trying to hold back a whimper. Her stomach lurched with every step of the person carrying her and she was having a hard time not throwing up. It was too much.

Her skin was burning up again and she called on her magic to cool herself. She needed to get away from the fire that was hurting her. She moved feebly, trying to get away.

"Shhhushh, you'll be in the water in a moment," a soothing voice said, but it hurt to listen. Her kelpie form was close to bursting out while her magic was trying to break free at the same time. She just wanted to give up and let them take over. There were two forces fighting inside of her and she didn't have the energy to do anything about it.

Another wave of pain crushed into her and this time, she couldn't help but whimper.

"Almost there, stay with me."

Such an easy thing to say, such a hard thing to do. Fire was burning through Macey's veins and made her scream out in pain. Her magic came without being called, but there was too much heat and not enough water. She could feel her skin sizzle and break into sores.

"Throw her in!"

A second later, she was home. Cool, gentle water hugging her from all sides, soothing the pain, clearing her mind. It still hurt, but the fog slowly dissipated, making it easier to think.

She was still being held, but she needed to shift, now. She struggled against the hold and this time, he let her go. She swam for an arm length before her kelpie broke free. She was too tired to even feel the pain of the shift. Her instincts took over and guided her through the change from human to kelpie. When water entered her scorched throat, she took a deep gulp, knowing that her gills would deal with it. To her surprise, the water was clean, not the chlorine soup it had been the last time. Someone must have refilled the pool with fresh water.

Her thoughts of gratitude disappeared when she could feel the webbing around her hooves build. She was ready to swim. With a whinny, she lept through the water, taking long strides, enjoying the feeling of her antenna being whipped back in the current. It was one of the most curious things about kelpies, that little appendage on their foreheads that nobody really knew what it was for. Some said it was connected to magic, but even kelpies without any magical abilities had an antenna. The only thing Macey knew was that it was extremely sensitive and ticklish. Her brothers used to chase her to then shake their manes against her head in the hope of making her squeal.

She slowed down when she started to think about her brothers. She still didn't know what was going on with them. And it didn't look like she'd find out anytime soon.

A hand touched her back and she whirled around, opening her maw, ready to attack. When she saw Jared swimming behind her, obviously not used to being in the water, her gaze softened. Her pain was almost gone and she could finally recognise her men again. One of them had carried her here. Who had been in the bedroom with her? Jared. Where were the other two? Were they safe? Did the Voice take them?

Panicked, she swam to the surface, looking

around the room. There they were, sitting on the rim of the pool, looking at her in worry. Her mind was swirling. She still wasn't back to normal. She'd been hurt this time, injured inside. She knew that Voice had broken something in her. The pain may have gone, but that didn't mean that everything was alright.

15

Even swaddled in a blanket, with Flint's arms wrapped around her, Macey couldn't stop shivering. She leaned back against him and his arms tightened. "Do you need more?" he asked softly.

"Please." She nodded, not caring how weak she appeared at that moment. She felt Flint heat up around her, his body temperature rising in an attempt to warm her up and stop the shivers.

Except, it wouldn't work, and they all knew it. While she might not be shivering from the cold, she still appreciated the warmth he was giving off, and the mere feel of him against her was making her feel far less alone.

"What happened?" Cam asked, crouching down in front of the pair of them. Concern was blaring in his eyes, but he kept his voice and demeanour calm.

She was grateful for that. She was a mess, and Jared had stormed off as soon as he'd known she was okay. Probably so he could hit something if the look on his face had been anything to go by.

"The Voice," she answered simply, shivering again. By the waves, she was grateful for Flint's arms around her and the steady beating of his heart. She breathed in and out slowly, trying to match the tempo of her breathing to Flint's. Maybe then she'd be able to rest and regain some of her strength, both physical from her shift, and mental from the walls the Voice had broken down. She hadn't even realised the latter was possible until today. She'd thought her mind was stronger.

"It's our fault," Flint said softly, his words cracking with unvoiced emotions. "I'm so sorry, Macey."

She lifted her hand and placed it on his, giving it a quick squeeze. "No," she said, shaking her head for emphasis. She hated the thought of him blaming himself. None of this was any of their faults. They were born to be the Wardens, at least, if Malan was telling the truth they were. And they were replacing the old ones in the process. Macey grimaced. It seemed to be a lot of effort to go to for them all just to be replaced in another hundred years or so. Then again, Flint and Cam had already admitted being centuries old, and she had no idea how old Jared was. For all she knew, he could be over a thousand and really look like a crippled man. She was grateful the latter wasn't true, as shallow as that made her feel.

"It might be, Macey," Cam said soothingly. "We lowered your walls when we..."

"But you also unleashed my magic," she pointed out, letting go of Flint's hand and holding her palm out, facing upwards. She called on the water deep inside her and summoned it to form a small fountain of water. Concentrating harder than she had to, she made the water dance in plumes around her hand, diving and twisting around. It was a weird experience. On the one hand, she could feel more power bubbling up inside her than ever before, and yet, it was taking more effort than ever to actually control it. She wondered if that was to do with her connection to the men. Maybe their own elements were diluting hers? Or maybe it was just the far more likely explanation of them being blocked by the damage the Voice had done.

If she ever got hold of him...

"Macey, are you okay?" Cam touched her face, his fingertips trailing gently over her cheek and sending tingles through her. This was worth all the agony.

"Lost in thought," she replied, her voice taking on a dreamy quality. She almost zoned out again, before remembering she couldn't without worrying Cam and Flint.

"We get that," Flint acknowledged in her ear.

"Is Jared okay?" she asked, meeting Cam's swirling grey eyes.

"He will be, yes. He's just very protective of you, and seeing you in pain...it was difficult for him." A thoughtful look crossed Cam's face. "It's difficult for us all, Macey. We weren't exactly expecting you, but now you're here..."

"You're our one," Flint finished for him.

"I am?" she squeaked, swallowing past the lump in her throat. They were getting to her. But this time, they were warming her from the inside. Swelling her heart to an abnormal size. Macey leaned forward, placing a hand on Cam's cheek. She took one of Flint's hands in her other one and squeezed tightly.

"Yes," Cam said softly.

"Yes," Flint echoed.

"What about Jared?" she asked tentatively, voicing one of the thoughts that'd been playing on her mind. Surely they shouldn't just be okay with this, and yet...

"You're his one too," Flint supplied, chuckling lightly. "You must be, or he'd never be acting like this." He released his hand from hers and waved it in the direction of the door where she assumed Jared must be.

"He wouldn't be rejecting sex, either," Cam added.

"That's true, I've never seen him do that before."

"But I thought he was starving himself..." she started, trying to make sense of it in her mind. He'd been starved, there was no doubt about that. So what was with what the guys were saying?

"He was, but he was doing that by avoiding sex, not refusing it," Flint explained, wrapping his arms back around her waist and pulling her back into him.

"Isn't that the same thing?" she muttered, really not seeing the nuance that he obviously did.

"Not at all. If you know food is in the kitchen, but you choose not to eat it even if you're hungry, that's starving yourself. If I said, 'want to eat this waffle?' and you said no, then that'd be you refusing," Cam explained patiently.

"Who'd refuse a waffle though?" she asked, laughing lightly. Relief flashed across Cam's face at the sound, though he didn't drop his calm veneer.

"Only someone that real-" He stopped talking suddenly, and Macey cocked her head to the side, wondering what he'd been about to say. Or more accurately, thinking she knew, but wanting some confirmation.

"Jared? Or you?" She studied his face intently for a reaction, but Cam seemed far too good at concealing his emotions.

"I think he's speaking for all of us," Flint answered instead.

"So now that we're bonded, you can all take the waffle?" Macey asked hesitantly, deciding to stick to the metaphor, even though it was making her hungry.

Cam chuckled. "If the waffle still wants us."

Macey smiled despite the shivers still racking her body. "I believe she does. Although if you eat her, won't she disappear?"

"Oh to hell with the waffle," Cam growled and pulled her forwards, out of Flint's lap, kissing her hard. She melted into his touch, letting his kiss carry her away, distracting her from the echo of pain resonating in her mind. She was weak at the moment, but with the guys around, she was safe. Now they just had to make sure the other Wardens were safe as well.

She held onto that thought until her lips left Cam's and he let her sink back into Flint's arms.

"The Voice, he said that Lightning and Ice are a couple. And that he's going to have both of them tomorrow. We need to do something about that."

She tried to hide her relief that the other female Warden was already in a relationship. Despite knowing that the three men were hers, it would help avoid any tension and jealousy. She'd never admit it, but she could be jealous and irrational sometimes. Especially now that she was bonded. Even the thought of someone else being interested in her guys made her growl.

"Are you still in pain?" Flint asked worriedly and she quickly shook her head.

"No, just cold. First I was burning, now I'm too

cold, what's next? Why is this happening? It doesn't make sense for my body to react this way, he only attacked my mind after all. How could he affect my body from far away?"

Cam cleared his throat. "We don't actually know if he's far away. He could be just around the corner. We have no idea what or who he is, and that scares me."

"Me too," Macey admitted. "But we need to warn Ice that he's walking into a trap. The Voice said he only needs four of us, and he's already got a hold on me. I don't know if I can resist him next time... Then he'd have three of us." She took their hands. "If he takes me, promise me you will run. He can't take you as well. Run and find Air, then hide. Whatever he's planning is bad, and we need to stop him."

Cam shook his head. "You know we couldn't do that," he said sadly. "We're bonded now, we'll never leave you. If he takes you, which we won't let him do in the first place, we'll come and get you back. You're our waffle and we'll fight for you."

Macey sighed. It was sweet of them, really, and she immediately felt warmer at the thought of having them all look out for her. But she couldn't put them in danger. She wasn't worth them getting hurt. But how could she prevent them from rushing after her? Deep inside, she knew that the Voice would be able to overpower her. She didn't stand a chance; her mind was weakened and her powers unreliable. It was only a matter of time... unless they managed to get to him first.

"Let's get Jared, we need to brainstorm," she said. Cam got up immediately and left the room. "Flint, can you make it warmer?"

"Your skin is warm, sweetie, if I make it any warmer you'll get a fever. I don't think it's a cold I can do much about." Despite his words, the flames in the fireplace grew in size and the crackling of the wood became louder.

"Urgh, I hope this won't last much longer. I don't like feeling this weak."

"You're not weak. You're the strongest waffle I know."

She laughed, giving him a gentle shove with her elbows. "Stop the waffle talk. It makes me hungry."

"Should I get us some food?"

"No, don't leave," she said, grabbing his hand for emphasis.

He was quiet for a moment, then said, "Cam is going to get us some."

"Nifty trick, your mind talking. Can you always hear each other's thoughts?"

Flint chuckled. "That would be awful. No, we send messages to each other, just like talking. Sometimes a few emotions get transmitted as well, but we're practised enough to shut them out."

"I always forget how old you two are," Macey mumbled. She wasn't going to say that it also made her slightly uncomfortable. How many girlfriends would they have had over the centuries? Did they see her as naive?

Jared's return saved her from those depressing thoughts. He knelt in front of her, his eyes wild as he scanned her from top to toe. "How are you?"

"I'm fine," she lied, knowing he was upset already.

"Don't lie to me. Never, ever, lie to me about how you feel. Understood?"

The undertone in his voice made her shiver. He was dead serious about this. He really cared, almost too much.

"Okay," she whispered and his expression softened. "I'm still cold and exhausted. I feel weaker than usual, like something's been taken away from me." Realising how pathetic that made her sound, she added, "But my magic is back and stronger than before."

"Good, now you're honest. Cam told me what you said about Lightning and Ice. I agree we need to get to Ice before Mahoun does." Macey shuddered at that name. She much preferred calling him the Voice. Naming a thing gave it power, and she felt like he had already a lot of that.

"Questions is, how?" Cam said, entering the room with a tray. When he noticed Macey's greedy looks, he shrugged. "Just some beans with toast. Didn't want to spend any time cooking. We've got more important things to do."

She didn't have a problem with beans on toast. Not at all. When he handed her a plate, she noticed that he'd buttered the bread before pouring the beans on top. Perfect. She was going to keep him.

"The blue men told us to go see the Sìth. Malan said to bond and then look for the other three Wardens. I vote for Malan's advice," Jared said before taking a big bite of bean-encrusted toast.

"Seconded," Flint agreed. "I definitely don't want to visit the Fae anytime soon."

"Thirded," Cam said and sat down next to Macey. She noticed how they were all sitting very close to her rather than in a circle as they usually did.

"Fourthed? Whatever the word is," she shrugged. "That doesn't answer the question of how we actually do that, though."

"I'm hoping the Staran might help us," Flint suggested. "It has taken us to where we needed to be in the past, maybe it will do the same again. Somehow this is all connected to the Staran and if they want us to heal them, they better show us where to find the other Wardens."

"Do you think they're strong enough?" Macey asked.

"Only one way to find out."

MACEY WAS GETTING a little bit fed up of staring into the Staran, though at least it meant she could curl herself around Cam or Flint and feel their body pressed against hers. Now she had other experiences of that, she could enjoy the Staran even more.

"Are we really just going to trust that they take us where we need to go?" she half-whined, despite knowing that it *was* the best plan they had. Really, it was the only plan they had.

"Do you have a better idea?" Jared asked, seeming surprisingly laid back given his refusal to hang around earlier.

"Well, no..."

"Then this is what we have to do," he pointed out, taking a step closer to Cam. She was grateful, she could use Flint's warmth still, even if she wasn't cold cold.

"But you're sure it'll take us where we need to go?"

"Of course not," Flint said, laughing. "When has it ever quite done what it was supposed to?"

He had a point. Not that it helped matters at all. Rather, it only helped increase the worry making itself known in the pit of Macey's stomach. Stupid Staran. Stupid Warden duties. Why couldn't she just have a nice quiet evening in with her men? They could eat good food, but only if Cam was cooking, and laze about in the pool. They'd all seen her kelpie form now anyway, so she could even shift and swim with them.

Of course, if she stayed in human form, there were other things she could do with the three of them in a pool. Things that would most definitely be fun. Images of wet skin sliding against wet skin assailed her, along with gasps and sighs of ecstasy. She wondered what being with all three of them would be like. Exhilarating most likely. Not to mention exciting and enticing. Though just how much convincing they'd need before they followed through with her desires, she didn't know.

"Earth to Macey," Flint said, waving his hand in front of her face.

"I thought that was Jared?" she threw back with a grin. He laughed aloud, quickly followed by Jared. Cam gave the three of them a stern look, as if to say they were supposed to be being sensible right at this moment in time. The glint in his eye gave him away though, he was as amused as the rest of them by Macey's quip. She wasn't sure why though, it hadn't been that good. She'd even go as far as saying it was cringe-worthy. But they all needed the light relief the joke would bring.

"It's not Earth I'll be bringing you back to," Jared said after he'd finished laughing, tipping her a wink.

"Alright, time to get serious now," Cam said sternly, his voice sending tingles through Macey. She hoped he had some other uses for that voice too. She could certainly think of a few ideas.

"Alright, okay," she acknowledged, her laughter fading to a stop. "But don't pretend you didn't need the comic relief."

She left Flint's side and made her way to Cam, going up onto her tiptoes and wrapping her arms around his neck. He leaned down and kissed her gently, confirming the same emotions they'd been talking about earlier. While none of them had voiced them out loud, she was pretty sure they all knew them to be true. She bore the marks on her back to confirm that.

She pulled back, smiling softly at him, a look that he returned without hesitation.

"Okay, now I'm ready to go." She unwrapped herself from him and made her way back to Flint, who held a hand out to her, using it to tug her forward and into his arms.

Closing her eyes and praying this trip wouldn't be as bad as some of the others, she waited as the familiar tugging feeling of the Staran took over once again.

She scowled. The landings didn't seem to be getting any easier, which was just a pain in the tail considering they'd still have to use the Staran to get around.

Macey glanced around, trying to make sense of where they were. It was almost like the mists around the guys' house. Hazy, and not at all conducive to being able to tell where they were.

"Did it work?" Jared asked, letting go of Cam as quickly possible.

She smothered a giggle. Guess they weren't getting up to any fun together then. That was a little disappointing, but so long as they still both paid attention to her, she didn't mind too much.

"Give it a second, and we'll see," Cam replied, a thoughtful expression crossing his face.

"Not through this mist we won't," Flint muttered. Macey smothered a giggle. He did have a point. The mist was thick, and only getting thicker.

"Really, Flint?" Cam scowled but didn't look away from the mists. Maybe he was as uneasy about them as Macey was. Flint slipped his hand around hers and squeezed tightly, for which she was more than grateful. She needed it. There was something extra eerie about these mists.

"You don't think the Sith are causing them, do you?" she asked, shivering. Was it her, or were things getting colder around here?

"I wouldn't have thought so," Cam said.

The four of them stood in silence, staring into the mists, and not wanting to take a step further. Macey saw a dark shape in the corner of her eye, and swivelled slightly on the balls of her feet, hoping it was just her on edge imagination, and not actually anything to worry about. To her horror, the shape didn't disappear at all. On the contrary. It almost appeared to be getting bigger, as if it was something coming towards them.

The mists around them cooled drastically, and Macey's breath began to frost in front of her. Letting go of Flint's hand, she hugged her arms around herself, wishing for the warmth of the living room they'd not long left behind. Flint was warm but she didn't want to look too needy right now, so better not to hold his hand as if she was afraid.

The shape became clearer, meaning it had to be something real, and not in her mind. That was never good.

"Cam..."

"Yes?" he replied instantly.

"What is it?" Her voice shook, which she hated. Weakness really wasn't something she liked, and at the moment she felt she was exhibiting far more of it than she should be doing.

"It's..." he trailed off as the shape emerged from the mists, along with what appeared to be a light shimmer of ice crystals through the air. Macey stepped back so she was pressed against Flint's chest, his warmth seeping into her, but still not quite enough to dispel the cold lingering in the air.

The shape, or rather, the cat, that appeared from the mists was large, probably at least half Macey's size, with jet black fur and a splash of white across its chest. But the thing that really caught her attention, was its eyes. They glowed an icy blue. Actually *glowed*. Considering she lived in a world filled with magic, she was still surprised by the glow. It was unnatural, and more than a little mesmerising.

"Hi," she blurted, unsure of why she'd suddenly decided to start talking to the cat. But something made her do it, and if there was one thing she'd learned over the past few days, it was that, sometimes, she should probably trust her gut instincts.

The cat nodded.

Wait. Nodded? Cats didn't nod, did they? She frowned at the creature, but before she could say anything else, it began to transform before her eyes. A tall, very pale, man with the same ice blue eyes, stood before her. His hair was the same colour as the cat had been, but with one white streak travelling through it. The similarities were striking, and she found herself just as enthralled by the man in front of her. He held out a hand to them, as if he was beckoning them to him.

"Can we help?" Jared asked cautiously, stepping slightly closer so he was flanking Flint and Macey, as Cam did the same on the other side.

"I hope so," the man replied, his voice surprisingly musical.

"How?" Flint asked, his voice rumbling in Macey's ear. She decided she could get used to their protectiveness. It made her feel a little warm and fuzzy inside.

"Please, help me save my sister," the cat-man replied.

"Your sister?" Macey asked, realising that she was once again the one speaking for all of them. Maybe that was her role in the Warden dynamic. Maybe her diplomacy training hadn't been for naught after all.

"She's dying. I asked the Staran for help and you arrived. Please, make her better."

For someone looking like an adult, his language was surprisingly simple. Maybe he wasn't used to being in his human form? Macey knew that from some older kelpies who refused to even half-shift. Their thought processes would change, become more kelpie, more primal.

"I'm not quite sure what we could do for her... none of us are doctors," she said, feeling terrible about having to disappoint him. He was as sad as he was good looking.

"If the Staran sent you, you will be able to help. Everything happens for a reason. Come, follow me." Without even waiting for a reply, he turned and walked away with the elegance of a cat.

"I don't like this," Cam muttered. "He's a cat sìth, they're not known for their trustworthiness."

"A cat fae? Really? I thought they were just a legend. Nine lives, black cats being unlucky, cat sìth stealing souls and all that..." Macey should really stop at being surprised that most myths seemed to be true. She was wondering why her grandmother never said that all the beings from her stories really existed. Surely, she would have known that?

"Incubi aren't trusted either, and here I am, a Warden," Jared said. "Let's follow him, and if he means us ill, we outnumber him."

"You don't know that, there could be more of them," Cam replied, but Macey ignored him.

"He wants our help, so let's see if we can be of assistance." She walked into the mists, following the cat-man, not waiting for her men. They would come with her, even if just to protect her. She realised that she could use their instinctive protectiveness to make them do what she wanted... fun.

Cam continued to whisper doubts and complaints, but Macey left him behind, catching up with the cat sìth.

"What is your name?" she asked him and he gave her a curious look with his glowing eyes.

"Us sìth never reveal our names, did you not know that?"

"Ehm, you're the first cat sìth I've met. Why not?"

"A name gives you power over the named. That's why we have nine, one each for partners, children, parents, family, neighbours, friends, colleagues, strangers and enemies."

"Wow, that must be hard to keep up with," Macey said wide-eyed. She was terrible with names, and remembering nine of them for each person would be more than a challenge.

"So you can't tell me your name for strangers?"

"No," he said simply, not giving an explanation.

"Well, I'm Macey. Nice to meet you."

"Nice to meet you too, Kelpie."

She sighed. "Why does everybody always know what I am and I have no clue about what they are?"

Cat-man chuckled. "I'm a cat. My sense of smell is excellent."

"Have you smelled many kelpies?" Macey asked incredulously.

"You're the first. But you smell like the sea, and you're not blue and don't have a fishtail, so kelpie was the logical option."

"Oh."

"We're almost there," he said and they walked in silence, Macey still pondering what she smelled like. Maybe she should ask the guys if she smelled fishy? Then she'd have to do something about it.

A growl that was distinctively non-cat carried through the mist. She stopped in her tracks, suddenly suspicious.

"Why did that sound like a dog? You said we're going to see your sister."

"We are. We're twins, in fact, but fraternal. She's not a cat sìth, she's a cù sìth."

"A what?"

He sighed. "A dog fae, if you wish. I got the whiskers, she got the wagging tail."

"Does that mean one of your parents was a dog and one a cat?" Macey had to suppress a giggle at the thought.

"Yes. Now will you please come? She needs help."

Macey turned serious immediately. "Of course. Although I still don't know what we could do."

"Neither do I," Cam muttered from behind her. The guys had been so quiet that Macey had almost forgotten all about them. The cat-man's voice was so alluring, so beautiful that her entire focus had been on him. Only Jared's incubus vibe got anywhere close to his.

Another growl, much closer this time. The mists slowly parted in front of them and offered them a view of an iron-wrought park bench. It looked out of place, as if it had been transported from an old-fashioned park. The ground was covered in mist, giving it an eerie, out-of-this-world feel. That made her think that she had no idea about where they were. Was this Earth? Another planet? An in-between place?

A heart-wrenching whine made her forget all about it. Behind the bench lay a large, white shape, camouflaged well against the misty background. It was too big to be a normal dog and far too white. Not even huskies were that white.

"Sister, I brought help," cat-man said and quickly walked around the bench, kneeling next to his twin. Cautiously, Macey followed him, flanked by Cam and Flint. The dog was massive, the size of a small bull. Her fur was snow white with a dark patch on her chest. Her eyes were the same glowing ones her brother had, but hers were red-rimmed as if she'd been crying too much. Her large tail had been braided and embellished with a bright pink ribbon. The rest of her fur was shaggy though, as if it hadn't been cleaned in a while.

She lifted a massive paw in greeting, but it was a weak gesture and it was obvious that she was finding it hard to move.

Macey approached carefully. The dog may have been poorly, but it was big and rather intimidating. She'd never been a fan of dogs, she was more of a cat person. And this cù sìth was far too big for her liking.

"What's wrong with her?" she asked and cat-man sighed.

"She was stupid and tried to protect a human. She says he was important, but how could a human be worth getting hurt?" The disgust was clear in his voice.

"Who did she protect him from?"

Cat-man frowned. "We do not say his name. But he is the worst of the evil spirits that roam this land. He can fill you with terror and his voice makes even the bravest afraid."

Macey turned around and looked at her men who were all having the same expression. The Voice. Could it be him? Could he have hurt the dog-woman?

"What did he do to her?"

"He sent her horrible images, memories filled

with dread, visions of terrible futures. Her mind is in pain and I cannot reach her. She's not getting out of the haze he induced. It's like she's trapped in a nightmare while awake."

That sounded more and more like the Voice.

"Can she talk?"

"She has moments where her mind is clear enough to communicate, but those are rare. I've had to piece together what happened."

"What happened to the human?"

"How should I know? And if I knew, I'd likely go after him. My sister is hurt because he got in trouble. He deserves to suffer for that."

Cat-man's eyes were glowing brightly now and Macey shrunk back at the anger shining in them.

A comforting hand pressed against her back. *Cam*. She leaned back slightly, wordlessly acknowledging his support. She liked that about her men. They were there, no matter what, offering her the support and protection she needed, while letting her fight her own battles. Though she wasn't naive enough to think they wouldn't insist on standing in front of her if her life was actually at risk. The foolish men. She could take care of herself. Not that flinching away from the cat sìth showed that.

In fact, she was being rude. The Cat-Man clearly loved his sister, so being angry and protective was only to be expected. She'd be exactly the same if it was one of her brothers who was injured and in pain. She pushed all thoughts of her brothers aside. There'd still been no way of knowing quite how involved they were in what was happening to her, and she didn't want to entertain the notion of their guilt any more than she had to. It'd only make her doubt everyone around her.

Instead, she reached out and touched Cat-Man's arm gently, her hand cooling drastically, same as it warmed when she touched Flint or he touched her. Her eyes unfocused as something unnamed flowed through her. It was an odd feeling, like she was solely focused on Cat-Man, but not focused on anything else at all. His pale blue eyes met hers, and they softened instantly.

"The man's not worth it," she said softly.

"I know," Cat-Man acknowledged. "That doesn't stop me wanting to rip him apart," he added slowly. Macey nodded once, understanding now creeping over her. She didn't think he'd actually hurt anyone unless there was a good reason to.

"How can I help?" she asked him, taking a step closer to him and feeling the cold rush over her. She felt oddly comfortable. Then again, the bottom of the loch was pretty cold, so maybe she was just used to it. She didn't think so though.

"I don't know. I was hoping..." He looked away, and uneasy look crossed his face.

"This will only work if you talk to me," she pointed out. "No matter how bizarre it might sound, I've probably encountered worse." She thought back over the events leading to this moment. Yes, she'd definitely encountered worse.

"I'd hoped you could connect minds with her." He glanced back at her as he finished his request, a hopeful but unsteady look in his eyes. Macey frowned. She didn't think she was unapproachable. She certainly hoped she wasn't.

"What makes you think I can do that?" She certainly had her doubts after all. She'd never had those kinds of powers. She didn't know many people who did. And she was sure she'd have discovered them by now, especially as Flint and Cam both had them.

"You've been spoken to by *him*." Cat-Man shuddered as he said the word. She didn't blame him.

"I call him the Voice," she supplied, barely holding off a shudder of her own just thinking that much about the invasion into her mind. Of all the things that could ever be done to her, that was the biggest violation anyone could have made. "But how do you know that?"

"I begged the Staran to bring me someone who knew. I had to speak his name to even get you here, and I worry that even that brief moment was enough to give him more power."

"Oh." She waited for a moment to see if he'd say anymore. "Your speech has improved massively." Her hands flew to her mouth as soon as the words had escaped. She couldn't believe she'd said that. How rude could she get? Behind her, Jared began to chuckle, and as pleased as she was that she could tell it was him just from the sound, it couldn't replace the shame she was feeling right now.

To her surprise, Cat-Man chuckled. "I'm not surprised, kelpie. I'm not a simpleton, but a long time in my other form takes its toll. When I regain my human shape, it sometimes takes a little conversation for me to return to my former self."

"Why don't you transform more often then?" It seemed like a very simple solution to his problem. More transformations meant more chances to practice speaking. That was all he needed really.

"I can't. I have a finite number of transformations. Once I return to my cat form for the ninth time, I will be stuck there forever."

"Or until you die?" she prompted. "That doesn't seem very fair."

"Life isn't fair, kelpie. But I think you know that better than anyone."

She nodded in reply, grateful for the silence of the others. It was more likely confusion and shock than anything else, but it was still good to know they trusted her judgement.

"How many more transformations do you have left?" she asked, hoping he said most of them.

"Two."

"Oh."

"Yes, it's a little concerning, but I had to do it for my sister's sake." He glanced at the large white dog, affection plain on his face. Right, yes, his sister. The reason he'd wanted Macey in the first place.

"May I?" she asked, indicating towards the large white form.

"Please."

She made her way over to the liveless dog's form. No, not dog. Woman. It was a woman and she needed to remember that. She crouched down next to her and pressed a gentle hand against where she imagined a dog's forehead was. Something almost crackled against her skin, but it was gone the moment it arrived, so Macey dismissed it.

"What do I do now?" she asked, feeling far more unsure of herself than was entirely pleasant.

"I don't know," Cat-Man replied.

"Follow your instincts, Macey," Cam insisted. She half-scowled at the unhelpful instructions, before realising he was probably right. He had been so far after all.

She drew in a long, deep breath, and pressed her hand more firmly against the woman's dog head. She pushed her thoughts out, trying to gain the woman's attention.

"It's not working," she grunted.

"Let me try and help," Cat-Man said softly, placing his hand over hers. The coldness of it sent shivers through her, but not unpleasant ones. There was definitely something enthralling about it, though what that was, Macey had no real clue. Maybe she'd unravel that someday. "Try again," he prompted.

She took another breath and squeezed her eyes back shut. This time, she felt a presence alongside her, and she reached out to it, feeling it touch the outskirts of her mind, but not probe within. Having connected with the presence that she was sure was Cat-Man, she pushed forward.

Hello? she thought out towards the woman. She even tried picturing her in her mind, but it was hard without a true frame of reference. *Hello?* she repeated.

Hi. The returning voice was weak but melodic, she liked it. But one thing it wasn't, was reassuring.

Can you tell me your name? she asked without thinking, cursing herself quietly when she remembered that wasn't something she was supposed to know.

Sharara, the weak voice replied. Macey's heart skipped a beat. That wasn't the answer she'd been expecting.

Sister! Cat-Man's scold sounded loud and clear

through Macey's mind. *That's not a name you should be telling. Especially in front of me.*

Shh, brother, you're giving me a headache, the voice answered.

A headache? You've had me worried sick, sister.

Macey found it interesting that he still wasn't using her name. Though what was it he'd said? They had different names for different people? She wondered which one Sharara had given her.

I'm sorry, I shouldn't have asked that, Macey said, trying to send as many apologetic thoughts as she could. She was slowly getting used to this talking-in-your-mind stuff. A lot of supernatural species seemed to do that. Strangely enough, kelpies didn't. Their language underwater was a mixture of whinnies and dolphin-like clicks. In Macey's opinion, their way of talking was a lot more sophisticated than how humans did it.

It's okay, you don't know our customs, Sharara answered weakly. *And I hate to say it, but I don't have much time left, I can feel the darkness approaching already.*

The darkness? Macey asked, wondering if the dog-woman was simply talking about losing consciousness.

He's keeping me trapped in a sphere of darkness. I'm in the middle of it and all I can see are memories. Bad ones. They replay on the walls of the sphere. When I'm out of there, I know that they're twisted and distorted, but not while I'm inside. And I don't get many lucid moments anymore; the walls are getting stronger and it's harder to escape.

How can I help?

I don't think you can. But the young man needs your help.

Sister, stop being so stupid! You're the one that needs saving, not that human. The cat-man's rage filled their conversation and Macey strengthened her mental barriers, making sure he wouldn't affect her. He definitely had anger issues, but that wasn't a surprise, really, when she thought about it. Cats weren't known for being rational.

I don't see a way out of here, Sharara said sadly. *But he is young, and his life is important. He was on his way to rescue his lady love...* She sighed dreamily. *It's so romantic.*

This isn't a fairy tale, sister. Snap out of it and come back to me! The desperation was clear in cat-man's voice.

I wish I could, dear brother. But I believe it's the end of my story. I cannot stay in this nightmare forever. Please, you know what to do.

Never. I'm not going to kill you. No chance! He was shouting now and Macey was tempted to intervene, but she could see how it was a conversation the two siblings needed to have.

Then let the kelpie do it. That's why you brought her here, right?

I... no, she's here to save you! That's why the Staran called her to me.

Kelpie, where were you headed? Sharara asked, finally including Macey back in the conversation.

It's a long story, but we need to find someone. Two people, in fact; one of them is imprisoned and the other one is on his way to rescue her. And I believe you may know one of them...

Cat-man growled. *No, we're not going to talk about the human. The Staran wouldn't do that to me... they brought you here to save her, not him... No, it cannot be. Sister, don't do this, I beg you!*

Sharara sighed. *I've lived long enough, brother. We both have. But if the kelpie and her companions are looking for this human, then we should help them. Let me do one good deed before my life expires. Let me send her my memories.*

I will have no part in this, cat-man growled. *You do it yourself, if you must, but I will not watch you die.*

I am too weak to do it on my own, Sharara whispered, her thoughts becoming weaker. *Please, brother. Please.*

The cat's anger dissipated in a flash, replaced by a deep sadness that made Macey shiver. She could feel tears running down her cheeks, far away, and was worried that her men might think she was in trouble. She hoped they wouldn't rip her out of her trance, or whatever else she was to call this.

Cat-man sighed deeply. *If I help you, will you try and*

stay a little while longer? Maybe if I go and fight... the Voice, it will free you.

Oh my sweet brother, I wouldn't have you sacrifice yourself for nothing. He is too strong. Stay with me in my last moments, help me go into the Beyond.

Macey wanted to leave them alone, but if there was any hope that Sharara had indeed seen Ice, she needed to stay. Finally, they were close to finding one of the other Wardens. And if they were lucky, Ice would lead them to Lightning. Then the only one left was Air, and then... well, what was going to happen then? Heal the Staran? Defeat the Voice? Live happily ever after? Somehow she was sure it wasn't going to be that easy.

Sharara interrupted her thoughts. *Kelpie, we will send you some of my memories. I will try and only send those related to the human, but it's not an exact science and you may get more than that. Fear not, it won't hurt.*

Okay, what do I need to do? Macey asked.

Relax, cat-man said in his most sultry voice and she could feel herself instantly grow calm. *Don't shy away, as she said, it's not going to hurt.*

Then, a flash of light hurtled towards Macey and before she could evade it, it crashed into her and she was thrown into whiteness.

～

THE MAN HAD bright blue hair and strange metal rings on his ears. Sharara stayed hidden in the mists, watching the human as he stumbled through her domain. He was the first human she'd seen in awhile. They rarely left Earth, and if they did, it was often involuntarily. There were some species who liked to keep humans as slaves. She shuddered. It was despicable to have another being as a slave, even if it was a human. And this particular one... she liked the bright colour of his hair. He was dressed in black, so the blue stood out even more.

He was limping slightly as if he'd been injured recently. But he looked determined as he made his way through the mists.

She was curious and moved forwards, careful to stay hidden. Her white fur made it easy; she'd always pitied her brother for having been born with black fur.

A hissing sound came from behind her and she whirled around just in time to evade a dark spear thrown at her. She growled loudly, warning whoever had attacked her that she was likely stronger than them. Cù sìth were not to be messed with.

A cry behind her made her turn around again. The blue-haired human was on the ground where he had thrown himself to not be pierced by the spear. Maybe it hadn't been intended for her after all. As she watched, the weapon dissolved into black mist.

She shivered. Only one being she knew could do such a thing. She was no match for him, and neither was the human. She should run away, but she was not a coward. She would stand her ground.

Another hissing sound warned her of another attack. She jumped through the air, out of the path of the spear and towards whoever had thrown in. She ran through the mists, hunting the assassin, but she didn't smell or see anyone. When she got to the place where the assailant would have had to have been to throw the spear at that angle, all she could see was a black circle etched into the ground. Tiny tendrils of black fog swirled around it, but there was no person in sight.

She growled in frustration and ran back to the human. He was no longer alone.

A dark figure was standing over his prone form, pinning him to the ground. He was doing something to the human, something that made her shudder. The evilness of it filled the air and she could hear the Staran groan in protest. The Staran rarely made a sound, they rarely got involved. This was a bad sign.

She needed to do something. She opened her mouth widely, exposing her razor-sharp teeth. Most enemies fled at that sight. She bellowed and the dark figure turned around, looking straight at her. He was surrounded by a cloak of dark mist, wavering in the air, throwing shadows over the man's face. All she could see were his piercing black eyes, shimmering like melanite.

They trapped her gaze, forced her to look at him. She couldn't turn her head, frozen in that moment, frozen in time. He approached her but she couldn't move, her eyes still fixed on his. The rumours were true, he could petrify with a single glance. How did she forget that? How could she be so stupid?

From the corner of her eyes, she could see the human get back up on his feet. At least it had been worth it. If he was clever, he would run and leave her to her fate. Human lives were so short, he deserved to live all of it.

A pain began to build behind her temples, quickly turning into a terrible headache. He was trying to break through her barriers, and he would soon reach his goal. She was physically strong, but not so much mentally. She tried to move her paws but her muscles didn't respond. He had her trapped. Panic began to bubble up in her mind. This was bad, really bad.

With a piercing push, similar to the black spear he had thrown before, he broke into her mind. Pain like nothing she had ever felt before rushed through her body and she screamed at the same time as he began to laugh.

Then the first memory appeared. Her mother, being torn apart by hunters. Her flesh flying through the air. Her wails as she slowly bled to death. Sharara whimpered, trying to close her eyes in the hope that it would make the memory go away. It didn't work.

More memories were thrown at her, more images of blood and terror. She had lived for centuries and there had been a lot of bad times in her life. Now, he was forcing her to look at it all.

While she was trapped in the memories, she could feel him build a prison around her. There was nothing she could do but watch as he locked her into her own mind.

Her last thought was that she had at least managed to save a life, even if it had cost her her own.

17

A blinding pain tore through Macey's head, not unlike the one that came before the Voice making an appearance. But she knew this one was different. Apparently, Sharara and Cat-Man had very different versions of something not hurting than she did.

Her vision cleared, and she could see the unmoving form of Sharara lying in front of her, barely moving. Cat-Man was watching over her, a drawn expression on his face. He clearly wasn't happy with the way things had gone then.

"She shouldn't have shown you that," he muttered darkly, his voice losing some of the alluring tone it'd held before. Maybe it was some kind of sìth trick. If he was related to *those* sìth, then it would make sense, but Macey really didn't know enough about either type of being to make that call.

"But she did," Macey pointed out. "And there's no changing that. All you can do is respect her wishes." She stood up tall and squared off against him. No way was he going to intimidate her into not respecting what Sharara wanted. Plus, this should lead her to Ice, and where she needed to be. It'd be good to actually have a name and face for the man she was referring to simply by his element. Same was true of Lightning and Air. Maybe Cat-Man was right. Names really did have power.

"But he..."

"It was your sister's choice to save him," she said, carefully avoiding the use of Sharara's name so as not to upset him further. He clearly hadn't liked that she knew it, so it seemed wise not to abuse that. "And as such, we should continue to protect him. For her sake. In her memory." She almost stamped her foot, but decided better of it. That probably wasn't the best way to gain his respect, which she wanted badly. She was royalty after all, and she needed to act that way.

"But..."

*Brother...*Sharara's weak voice resonated through Macey's mind and she grasped onto it. *Heed her, go with her. Your destiny lies that way.*

Sister...

Listen. I'm slipping more by each moment. Listen in the time I have left, don't argue.

Sharara sounded a little stronger to Macey, though that was probably just the case of sheer determination. Sharara was clearly desperate to get through to her brother. If only Macey could help, but it almost seemed like Cat-Man was adamant he'd dislike her.

Very well, sister. But only as it is frowned upon to deny the wishes of the fading.

She could hear Cat-Man sigh in her mind, and a following chuckle from Sharara. Despite the solemn occasion, Macey found herself smiling softly. She bet the two of them were at each other's throats when they were younger. She was also certain that Sharara was the one who'd won most of those battles.

Destiny, with the kelpie.

Yes, I got that bit, he responded, surprisingly dryly and Macey threw him a disapproving look. It didn't matter if he was talking to family, he shouldn't be taking that tone.

The one she seeks, she's not in a good way. She's worse than I am. Has been with him longer as a lure for the man I saved.

Cat-Man growled. Instead of flinching away, Macey calmly placed a hand on his arm, offering him the silent support she figured he needed. He calmed almost instantly, which was unexpected, but also a relief. The last thing she wanted was Sharara more upset, or for one of her men to intervene. Their version of that would likely end in pain. As it was, she imagined they were only staying as passive as they were because they trusted her and because she didn't seem to be in any danger. Hopefully, things would stay that way.

What's happened to Lightning? Macey asked when neither of the sìth beings said anything.

She's been locked up. But not just in her mind. Physically too. I dread to think what he's done to her. Sharara sounded sad, and Macey longed to pull her into her arms and hug her, offer the emotional support the other woman needed. Except that wasn't really a possibility right at that moment. It probably wouldn't ever be, given how fast she was fading.

*That sounds...*Macey started, unsure how to continue. It sounded horrific. She'd discovered first hand what the Voice was like when he was inside someone's head. And now she'd seen what more prolonged exposure could do. In fact, seeing Sharara added a new concern in her mind. Was this looking into the future for her? It was certainly looking into the past for Lightning if what the dog-woman said was true.

Horrifying?

*Dangerous. What happens if Lightning is...*She couldn't finish the thought. If Lightning was gone, and it was looking at least a little likely that she could be, then they could face some big problems. Like how to fulfil a prophecy she didn't even understand if they were missing a Warden. She erased the thought from her mind. She'd deal with that if and when it happened.

I don't know. There are rumours that a Warden can pass on their position, but only if they're at death's door. But they're only rumours.

How do you know about the Wardens? Macey asked. They'd made no mention of it before, and yet now it was a big thing, which was odd, to say the least.

Following Ibzan wasn't a complete waste. I learned plenty from watching the Ice Warden. Ma...the Voice isn't all that subtle in his demands. He knows who you are, Macey.

I'd guessed that much. The words slipped out, and Sharara laughed into her mind, the sound swiftly turning into a cough. Macey smoothed her hand down Sharara's back and the dog-woman seeming to relax slightly as she did. That was good, at least. Anything to make her more comfortable, especially since her breathing had become particularly ragged.

But he also knows what *you are. He knows you're the one who can stop him, and he wants your power for himself,* Sharara warned.

Can he really take my power?

You'd be surprised what he can do with a name, Cat-Man interrupted. *They hold power for a man like the Voice.*

And he knows mine. Dread washed through Macey. *Wait, is he....?*

I think so, but I don't know for sure. It was hard to get a good read on him through the blackness. She shivered under Macey's palm.

How do we find him? The question had been burning on the tip of her tongue since they'd arrived. Mostly because she'd been hoping this was the place they were meant to be. The place where Lightning was, and Ice would soon be. She really should know by now that even the best-laid plans went awry. Especially with the Staran involved. If she hadn't known better, she'd have thought the Staran were run by pixies looking for mischief.

I suspect he'll find you, Sharara responded instantly. *Though in case he doesn't, my brother will help guide you.*

What?! Both Macey and Cat-Man responded at the same time.

It is my dying request to you, brother. Guide her. Protect her. Aid her.

Aye, Cat-Man replied, seeming more than a little reluctant. Macey wasn't sure she blamed him. She was even starting to get the impression he wasn't her biggest fan, but that was probably more to do with the way his sister was being with her than anything else.

Can you leave us a second, brother?

Cat-Man frowned, clearly not a massive fan of the

idea. But he also nodded, and Macey felt his mind pull away from the two of theirs.

He's gone, she said needlessly.

Thanks, Sharara replied. *I have a gift for you.*

That's really not necessary, Macey said, feeling a little flustered.

You can't say no to a dying cù sìth, Macey. That'd just be rude.

Sorry, Macey murmured.

What I'm about to do can never be revealed to anyone but those you'd trust with your eternal life. We both know there are six of them. But no one else, understood?

Macey nodded, slightly confused. Sharara sucked in a deep breath, her body weakening beneath Macey's touch.

> *For my last act upon this earth,*
> *Before I head to my rebirth,*
> *I bequeath upon to thee,*
> *A name which comes in three.*
> *Macey must be the first,*
> *Reveal the second and be cursed,*
> *The third you shall obtain,*
> *When Seven Wardens shall reign.*

With her final words, Sharara took a deep shuddering breath and stilled. A tear slipped down Macey's face as the death, and the knowledge Sharara was imparting, overtook her. The rush of information through her mind, coupled with the intense emotions, was enough to send Macey reeling. Not quite sure what she was doing, she stumbled away from the still body of the dog-woman, and back towards her men. She hadn't taken more than three steps when blackness overtook, and she crumbled to the floor.

"IBZAN, HIS NAME IS IBZAN." Her voice was all weird and croaky, but it was important for them to know. They finally had a name.

"Whose name?" Cam asked, his hand cool on her forehead. All three men were looking down at her and her head appeared to be lying on Cam's lap.

"How long was I out?" She ignored his question, asking her own instead. They would figure it out.

"Only a few minutes. Are you alright?" Flint looked worried and she smiled to show that she was fine. And if she ignored the headache she was still feeling behind her eyes, she was perfectly fine.

"Yes, everything's alright. I got hit with a few memories, that's all. How is cat-man?"

Jared chuckled. "Did you just call him cat-man?"

Macey frowned. "What do you call him in your heads?"

The three men looked at each other. "Cat-man."

"See?" Macey smiled, before remembering what just happened. Sadness overcame her. "She's dead?"

Cam nodded, stroking her hair. "He's not said anything since he awoke a few minutes before you did. He's sitting with her and we've been waiting for you to wake up and tell us what's happened."

Macey sat up and shuffled back until she could lean against Cam's broad chest. "Ice. His name is Izban. The Voice was after him and Sharara - that's the dog woman - protected him. He's got blue hair and piercings, he looks like a punk. A very pretty punk, though."

"Hey, he's off limits," Flint warned, his tone only half joking.

"Don't worry, I'll admire him from a distance. If we ever find him. When the Voice attacked Sharara, Izban got away, but he was wounded. The cù sìth probably distracted the Voice long enough to give Ice a chance for escape, but if we're right, he'll run right back into his reach. He's on his way to Lightning, just as we thought. And she's in bad shape."

"How do you know that?" Cam asked, pulling her closer.

"The Voice told Sharara to taunt her, to show her that her sacrifice was for naught. That he'll have Ice soon anyway, and that he'll suffer together with his partner. I'm scared we may be too late for Lightning."

"But the prophecy says that Ice will free her," Flint protested. *"Lightning is trapped, Ice will break the chains."*

"Let's hope so," Macey said darkly. "I've felt the Voice in my head. I can't even imagine how it would be like to be under his influence for days, weeks, or longer. I'd go mad within hours. The pain... it was bad."

She shivered and Cam wrapped his arms around her, his lips leaving a trail of gentle kisses on her shoulders. Right now, her men were there for her, all three of them. But if the Voice came back, she'd be alone. She was weak, so she better not give him another chance. They needed to be the ones on the offensive.

"Sharara said that her brother might be able to help us find Izban," she said and almost smiled as she saw hope light up the guys' eyes.

"Do you think he'll do it?" Jared asked, casting a sceptical glance at the cat sìth who was cradling his sister's body.

"It was her last wish, so yes, I think he will do it. Doesn't mean that he won't complain every single step of the way. He was not happy that she shared her memories with me, nor that she put herself between Ice and the Voice. But I believe he'll come with us, even if only to honour his sister."

"Then we better hurry up before Lightning is hurt

even more," Cam said with determination and the others nodded their approval. There was no question that they needed to hurry. Only, how to find them? And even if they knew where the Voice was keeping Lightning and therefore where Ice was headed, it didn't mean they knew how to free them and get out of there alive.

Macey huffed. There were too many unanswered questions. She didn't like it.

"I think it should be you to ask him to leave," Flint said quietly and pointed towards the cat sìth. "You're the one he's talked to the most."

"Yeah, and the one he's growled at," she sighed, but she knew he was right. It had to be her.

She slowly approached the cat-man and kneeled down by his side. His ears twitched, but he didn't acknowledge her.

"Your sister said you'd be able to help us," Macey said softly, watching as the man's chest heaved and deflated. He was breathing hard, probably trying to hide his sobs. "There are lives in danger and you are the one to save them."

"I don't want to save a human," he whispered, "it's not worth it. They've hurt our kind so much, and now I'm supposed to help one of them? How can she ask that of me? How can *you* ask that?"

"I don't think he's a normal human," she said carefully. "He's one of the Seven Wardens, which means he has magic. We think that ice is his element and that he's on the way to save his partner, who commands lightning. We need them to heal the Staran, to..."

"You can heal the Staran?" he asked incredulously. "Nobody can do that. It's been foretold that it will die."

She shook her head, not even remotely taking that into consideration. "No, it won't die. There's a prophecy speaking of the Seven Wardens. Well, we are four of them. Your sister knew about us, and she knew that we needed to find the other three. Please, help us. If not for the Staran, then for your sister."

"I don't believe in prophecies," he grumbled. "But if he is indeed a mage... she must have known that." He sighed and got up, sadly looking down at Sharara's prone body. "I will help you find that boy. But that's all you can ask of me, I will not stay after."

"I wouldn't expect you to," Macey said softly. "We only need you to help us track him."

Squaring his shoulders, he turned around, finally offering her a look at his face. His glowing eyes were dim and red-rimmed from crying. She wanted to give him a hug, but knowing cats, he probably wouldn't like it.

Before she could say anymore, he walked away from the park bench, towards the clearing that

Macey had witnessed in Sharara's memory. The place where Izban had been attacked.

He walked around, inspecting the mist-covered ground.

"I will have to shift," he finally announced and Macey's heart beat hard in her chest.

"But you only have two changes left," she protested, but Cam put a hand on her shoulder.

"He knows that. We need him to do it."

"Once I've shifted, follow me. If we have to travel on the Staran, grab hold of me, but don't grip me too tight. Sometimes my cat instincts take over and I wouldn't want to hurt you."

In a smooth motion, the man turned into a big black cat. It was so different from Macey's shifts, so much more elegant and quick. It looked like no effort at all. But then, she shouldn't be jealous. She got to change forms as often as she wanted. He only had one left now.

The cat prowled from side to side of the clearing, sniffing the ground. Macey was beginning to doubt whether this was going to work, when he finally growled and ran off. The cat was large and fast and she was having trouble keeping up with it. The guys flanked her, with Jared at the rear as usual. The mists became thicker the further they ran and she already longed for the clearing they'd started from. She'd had enough of fog to last her a lifetime.

The mist was so thick that she almost bumped into the cat who had stopped and was waiting for them. He curled his tail and somehow, she knew it was time to travel on the Staran.

Macey looked at her men and they all followed him into the mists.

Cat Sìth

18

She couldn't see more than a foot or so in front of her, which worried her more than a little, but she had to trust Cat-Man. While he didn't really seem to like her, Sharara had put a lot of faith in him, and had asked him to help them. And if there was one thing she could definitely say about Cat-Man, it was that he loved, and trusted, his sister. She'd meant a lot to him.

Are you okay? she thought at him. She didn't know if it would work, but hoped so. All she might get in return was a growl, but she was willing to take that risk.

No, he replied after a silence that'd stretched just long enough for Macey to start doubting her attempts at communication had worked.

Is there anything I can do? she asked, softly.

Stop with the questions, he snapped. Something recoiled within Macey, hating the tone he was using even if she understood the why.

"Sorry," she muttered aloud, scared to think in his mind again.

The five of them continued into the thickening mists in silence. There was so much they needed to talk about. So much to plan. But something about doing so just felt wrong. It was potentially to do with Cat-Man's grief, but Macey wasn't so sure. To her, it felt far more likely to be something to do with the mistrust she held for the mists themselves. As stupid as it seemed to distrust a weather pattern. But the mists seemed to be linked to the Staran. They could even *be* the Staran as far as Macey was concerned. And while she didn't believe the Staran themselves were bad, something, or someone, had made them sick. And if they knew how to do that, then they probably knew how to hear and see through the mists.

If there was one thing Macey had learned recently, it was that anything was possible. And that if a story existed about something, then there was a good chance it existed somewhere in the world. Maybe not quite in the exact way the stories said, but certainly in some form.

Are you ready? Cat-Man's sudden reappearance in her head made her jump.

For what? she replied.

To travel the Staran, he said shortly. She could almost hear the 'duh' at the end. Except that he wasn't her brothers, and was centuries old, so wouldn't be as immature as to actually say it aloud. Or think it. Or whatever they were doing right now. All this magical communication would give Macey a headache if she had time to stop. Or if she didn't already suffer from magical headaches induced whenever the Voice made an appearance.

"Yes, I'm ready to travel the Staran," she said aloud, mostly for the men's benefits. She needed to remember how much she hated it when Cam and Flint talked in their heads, and that it probably felt the same for the three of them when she was talking to Cat-Man. Then again, it wasn't like she had a choice with Cat-Man. He couldn't exactly speak aloud in this form, and she couldn't ask him to transform back just so she could chat to him. She couldn't ask him to ever transform back for any reason. Not knowing it was the last time he could do so.

Thoughts flickered through her mind, mostly centred around if there was a way she could change his fate. To make it so he could shift any time he wanted. That ability wasn't something she'd ever given much thought to, but now it was the only thing on her mind. Maybe there were other things she took a little for granted too. She needed to watch that in future.

Cat-Man nodded his big black head, and before Macey had time to even think another word, she found herself being sucked back into the Staran and down their path to...wait, where were they going? No one had actually told her, other than that they were heading towards Ice. Maybe that was all there was to it. Maybe the Staran didn't just work on visiting a place, maybe visiting just a person was possible too, no matter where they were.

When they worked at all, anyway. As far as Macey could tell, the Staran very rarely actually did what they were supposed to. Or at least, not for her and her men they didn't. It was possible that the Staran just didn't like Wardens. Or that the person who'd made it sick in the first place had programmed it not to like Wardens. Programmed? Spelled? She couldn't work out the right word for it. Then again, the last thing she'd ever expected was to *have* to work out a word for a sick travel system. Life had certainly taken a very strange turn.

Without her being fully aware of it, Macey's feet found themselves on firm ground again. She frowned. That had been a lot smoother landing than just about every other trip she'd taken through the Staran. Unless she counted the first one, but she didn't. She'd been unconscious for that one, so it hardly counted.

"That was almost like it should be," Cam said, awe written all over his face.

Macey glanced around, surprised to see the mists were thin here, almost verging on non-existent. She lightened her grip on Cat-Man's fur but didn't move her hand away. She wasn't sure whether or not their connection would survive if they broke contact.

The advantage of having a Cat Sìth with you, he chuckled down the connection.

"Does it really make a difference to have you with us?" Macey asked aloud. She knew Cat-Man would hear her, and didn't want the other three cut out of the conversation.

Yes, if the damage to the Staran has been done by who I think it has.

"Cryptic," she muttered, before relaying back to the men. Flint took a step towards her and pulled her close with a firm hand on her waist. He pressed a kiss onto the top of her head, and she almost melted into him.

"We know the Voice is behind it anyway," Cam pointed out.

"Yes, but what is the Voice?"

He's like me, Cat-Man said, taking Macey a little off guard.

"A Cat Sìth?"

No, just of a fae line. But that's bad enough.

Yes, she imagined it was bad enough. The Voice seemed strong, particularly after what Sharara had said.

"But aren't we supposed to be with Ice?" she asked, looking around her for the first time. Unease settled in her stomach as she took in what looked like an abandoned warehouse looming in front of her. The lack of mists didn't even stop it from being eerie. Which said a lot. "Please tell me we don't have to go in there?" she asked of her men.

"I can tell you that, but I don't want to lie to you," Cam said.

"But we're with you, every step of the way," Jared added, coming to stand next to her.

"And Ice is in there?"

I don't know, but this is where the Staran brought me when I thought of his name. Cat-Man shrugged. Which in any other situation, may have been comical. As it stood, Macey wasn't overly amused.

"Are we on Earth?" Macey asked. With all the travelling and strange places she'd been to recently, it was hard to tell. It looked like a human warehouse in an abandoned industrial area. Most of the glass windows were broken, the rest covered in yellow dust. It could easily stand in as a crime scene in a film. It gave her the creeps.

At least she had her magic back, so she wasn't

defenceless. Neither were the others, and she was sure that Cat-Man had some decent claws on his furry paws. Then why did she feel such a level of hopelessness and despair? She was tempted to give up and run away, hide somewhere with her men, wait until the Voice found them and she invited it in...

Wait. Those weren't her thoughts. She was a kelpie princess, she wasn't going to run.

"Something's wrong," she whispered. "Do you feel it as well?"

"Darling, I want to feel all of you." Suddenly, Jared hugged her from behind, putting his hand on her boobs while whispering in her ear. "I'm going to take you here and now. You're the most delicious being I've ever tasted and I'm going to devour all of you. You're going to be my entree, dinner and dessert and when I'm done with you, there will be nothing left but a whimpering mess begging me for death."

She jumped out of his embrace, staring at him incredulously.

"What the waves did you just say? What's wrong with you?"

Jared ignored her and stalked towards Macey, his eyes crazed. This wasn't the Jared she knew, this was the incubus he kept locked inside.

As one, Cam and Flint stepped in front of her. "Stay back, he's not himself!" Flint shouted and flames appeared around his outstretched hands.

"Yeah, I kind of figured that out myself," Macey mumbles. "What's wrong with him?"

"You said you were feeling strange? It's the same for him. Except that he didn't manage to get himself out of the mental grip of whoever is doing this."

"I don't think it's the Voice," Macey said slowly. "It feels different. Less aggressive, more… sneaky. Almost playful. Teasing. A warning, but not a threat yet."

"Well, I'm not enjoying this game," Cam huffed as he kept a barrier of air between them and Jared who was now beating against it, trying to get to Macey. His expression was pure lust and no humanity was left in his eyes. No wonder incubi had such a bad reputation.

"How are you two not affected?" she asked, inspecting them carefully for any sign of Jared's madness.

"Centuries of practice. And with our mental abilities, we're used to keeping up strong barriers around our minds. It takes someone much stronger than this to break through those."

"And can you use these exceptional powers to make him normal again?" Macey asked drily, watching as Jared was ripping off his shirt, presenting his shapely abs to her. As if that would make her go over and touch him. Tempting, yes, but she preferred the normal Jared, not the crazed incubus version.

"Darling, come to me, I want to drown in your waters," Jared shouted, his voice the most alluring thing she'd ever heard. She took a step forward, towards the beautiful sound, but a hand on her shoulder stopped her.

She turned to Flint, breaking the spell. "Thanks."

"No problem. He's even making me want to go over and kiss him."

She stared at him. "Are you..."

"I've been known to experiment," he grinned and winked at her. An image of him in Jared's arms, their hot bodies entwined, fluttered into Macey's mind. Wow. Was that excitement she felt? Or jealousy? Or a mixture of both? But no, this was not the time for this. They needed to get their incubus back to normal so they could investigate the warehouse.

"Where's the cat?" Cam suddenly asked, looking around while still keeping up the barrier around Jared.

"He was here just a moment ago.... do you think it affected him, too?" Macey asked, but Flint shook his head.

"His mental strength is as least as good as ours, if not better. He'll be safe from the influence of whatever this is. But why didn't he say anything? It's odd for him to just disappear like that."

"Is it?" Cam asked. "He's not been very happy

about coming with us in the first place. Maybe he decided his job was done?"

"Look, I've got no trousers on!" Jared shouted, interrupting them. He was indeed only wearing his boxers now and was in the process of getting rid of those too. Macey cringed. As much as she liked seeing him naked, this was bad timing.

"Do something about him, please?" she begged the other two, covering her eyes.

"We could knock him out and see if he's normal again when he wakes up?" Cam suggested. "Or find some rope and chain him to that lamp post and hope that he's still there when we're done?"

Macey didn't like either of those options. "Or you stay out here with Jared and I'll go inside with Flint?"

Cam growled. "No way. We're all going together. We don't know what awaits us in there."

"Sweetheart, look how hard I am for you!" Macey whirled around, taking care not to look at his midsection.

"Oh for waves' sake, it's enough!" she shouted and threw a ball of water at him. She'd intended something small, but her magic decided otherwise and drenched Jared in a massive fountain of icy water. He squealed as it pushed him to the ground.

"Oops," she muttered, evaporating the rest of the water before it could actually hurt him.

Jared slowly got up on all fours. "Why am I wet?" he asked slowly? "And why the fuck am I naked?"

Cam grinned and released the wind barrier. "Good to have you back, mate."

Jared picked up his wet clothes and looked at them with confusion. "Did I go incubus?"

"Yes, you did. I think you have some apologising to do. Some of the stuff you said to Macey wasn't very polite," Flint chuckled and waved his hands through the air. A moment later, the clothes were dry again and Jared quickly slipped into them while hiding his blushing face.

"I'm sorry," he mumbled, clearly embarrassed. "I usually have it under control... was it very bad?"

Macey laughed. "You said you were going to have me for dinner."

"Oh. But I didn't...?"

"They stopped you before you got a little too touchy-feely," she explained and he breathed a sigh of relief.

"I can't believe this happened. It's been ages since I went full incubus. Anybody know what happened?"

"I'm pretty sure we're going to find out once we finally enter that warehouse," Macey said, a healthy dose of impatience in her voice. They'd lost too much time already. If Ice wasn't here, it had been a complete waste. And if he was, this chaotic mind fuck may have made everything a lot worse.

"Let's go," she said and walked towards the large metal doors. They were covered in dents and rust. Cam stepped in front of her and put a hand on the door handle.

"Ready?" he whispered and Macey looked around. Three determined men met her gaze and she squared her shoulders in advance. It was time to solve this mystery.

The entrance to the warehouse loomed above them, causing something like dread to flow through Macey. Her men were next to her though, and that made everything at least a little easier. Though she'd prefer it if she knew where Cat-Man had gotten to. Despite it all, she was feeling a little attached to the odd creature.

She took a step forward and gritted her teeth as the urge to shift forms overwhelmed her. She knew she couldn't give in though. She wouldn't be able to breathe if she did. Plus, she imagined kelpies were rather ungainly in their aquine form on land. There wasn't much grip for webbed hooves against a hard floor. A struggle began within as the shift tried to take hold. This wasn't good. She *couldn't* let the shift take hold, no matter what she did.

"You okay?" Cam asked, his normal calm, coolness cracking slightly as his worry shone through. Despite it all, Macey's heart skipped a beat. He was worried about her. *For* her. It was one thing knowing it, but quite another seeing it. She knew that was a silly thing to say, particularly when she bore his mark on her back, but even so.

"Just struggling against the magic," she said, nodding towards the warehouse.

Now do you understand why I'm not with you, Cat-Man said, making her jump. She hadn't expected him to still be about after his silence during the incubus attack. She didn't really blame him for leaving during that. Jared had been a sight to behold, that was for sure.

You're still here.

Of course, I promised my sister I'd help you. I can't break that promise just because one of your husbands gets out of control. Cat-Man sounded amused, filling Macey with relief. She knew he wasn't about to just get over his sister's death, but at least he wasn't in the place where he was ready to end himself over it all. Or give up on life completely and go on a rampage. She wasn't sure which was worse, though at least he wasn't still going on about killing Ice. No, not Ice, Izban. She knew his name, she should get used to using it.

Thank you, but they're not my husbands, she responded.

What do you think they are then?

Macey didn't respond. She couldn't. What were they to her? More than just a fling. More than just her boyfriends. But they weren't married...right? They'd need a ceremony for that. She pushed the thought away. She'd deal with that one when there wasn't a massive imposing warehouse to deal with.

I'll be waiting out here until you return, or the enchantment breaks. But I can't risk being forced to change forms. A wave of sadness washed over Macey, and she wondered whether it was Cat-Man's emotions, or whether it was her own reaction to what he was saying. Whatever it was, it distracted her from her concerns of just moments ago.

Of course, totally understandable.

Thank you, kelpie. His voice faded, almost like he was walking away. Though surely that shouldn't be possible? He was a disembodied voice in her head right now, walking away wasn't physically possible.

"Earth to Macey." Jared waved his hand in front of her face.

"She must be really out of it if she's not calling you an idiot over that pun," Flint deadpanned and she looked at him to find an amused smile gracing his face. It didn't quite cover the seriousness in his eyes as he studied her though.

"Sorry, I was talking to Cat-Man."

"He's still about then?" Flint raised an eyebrow. If she wasn't so preoccupied, she might have worried about the hint of jealousy in his tone, but as it was, she was still fighting slightly with her inner kelpie.

"Yes, he can't risk a shift though." Nor could she

ask him to. That wasn't her place. "You ready?" she asked her men.

"It's you we're waiting on, Princess," Jared said with a laugh. Macey spun on her heels and stared him down.

"Don't call me Princess," she insisted, her face set into hard lines.

"But you are one?" He didn't seem to quite be getting how serious she was.

"Yes. And I've been treated as one since the day I was born. Except for here, except for now. Can we *please* keep it that way? I'm just a woman, that's all I want to be." Her voice trembled at the end, and she had to blink back some of the tears that were form-ing. By the waves, what was wrong with her? She was never this emotional.

"You're hardly *just* a woman, Macey," Cam said softly in her ear as he wrapped his arms around her waist and pulled her back into him. He kissed her cheek as she pushed herself back into him further. "You're our waffle at the very least," he pointed out with a chuckle.

"Stop it with the bloody waffles already, you're making me hungry," she half-laughed, half-cried.

Macey extracted herself from Cam's arms and reached out to give both Flint and Jared's hands a squeeze. She didn't want them feeling left out.

"Okay, I'm actually ready this time."

She faced the warehouse entrance and focused on keeping her kelpie completely under control. She wasn't happy about it, and Macey could feel her whinnying away within her chest, but there was no alternative. Not without causing a flood of Noah-like proportions, anyway. Putting one step in front of the other, she moved into the gloom.

Cu Sìth

19

I t was just as gloomy inside the warehouse, but there was one big difference: there were a lot of flashing lights. Macey tried to time them in her head, but failed each and every time. There didn't seem to be any kind of rhyme or reason to the gaps between the flashes. Probably because they had nothing to do with the clearly frayed wiring about the place. If she had to take her guess, the electricity hadn't been working here in a good while.

And that was without mentioning the smell. It was damp. But not the good damp she liked. This was a damp rotting smell, the one that permeated everything and made whoever could smell it want a ridiculously hot shower in which they could scrape off layers of skin. Safe to say she was burning these clothes when she got a chance. It was a good thing her men lived in a magically enchanted house that could provide what they needed. Between them, and everything that kept happening, she seemed to be going through clothes like they were going out of fashion. She tittered to herself. Maybe they *were* going out of fashion, and this was the universe's way of telling her as much.

She covered her mouth with her hand. This really wasn't the place to be making a lot of noise. Not until they were sure of who was in here. And at the moment, she was clueless beyond the fact there was *someone*. There had to be, or else there wouldn't be an enchantment on the outside of the warehouse. If she kept telling herself that, then she might even start believing it.

"Flint, you go right, Jared, you're left. Macey, with me," Cam whispered and the other two men disappeared into the shadows. Carefully, she and Cam continued further into the warehouse. Macey felt exposed, walking in the centre of the great empty space, and the mysterious flashes didn't help make her feel any more reassured. Her eyes were starting to hurt from all the light and she noticed she was blinking a lot. If whoever was here was trying to distract them, they were doing a great job.

The other end of the warehouse was drenched in darkness; for some reason, the flashing lights stopped halfway there. For once, Macey was preferring the darkness to light. They continued to walk further, looking around for any clue of who might be here. This place couldn't be as empty as it seemed, it didn't make sense. The Staran had brought them here for a reason. But why couldn't this adventure come with instructions? There was a lot of guessing and wondering recently. Macey liked cold, hard facts, as cold as the water she had grown up in and as hard as.... better stop there.

When they had almost reached the end of the flashing lights, Cam put a hand on her shoulder. "Let me go first," he whispered and grudgingly, Macey let him. There was no point in arguing, his stoic expression told her that.

While Cam tiptoed into the darkness, Macey looked around for a sign of the other two. Nothing. They were either excellent at hiding or something bad had happened. But surely they would have made some kind of noise? Screamed? Yes, it had to be the first option.

Warily, she stepped from one foot onto the other. Cam had disappeared into the dark shadows in front of her and she was left here, alone, not sure what to do. He said he'd go first, but not that she shouldn't follow... right?

She smiled tensely and walked into the darkness.

Which suddenly wasn't dark anymore. It was like a curtain had been opened and she now had a clear view of the stage. It was chaotic, to say the least. A lone, cloaked figure was standing in a circle of flames about ten metres away from her. His back was turned to her and judging from his frantic movements, he hadn't noticed her approach. He was flailing his arms up and down as if to extinguish the flames.

Bright lights were flashing all around him; the same kind she'd seen at the front of the warehouse. They didn't originate from anything, they were like little lightning bolts racing through the air.

Lightning. Surely not? No, Lightning was a woman, and this was definitely a man.

The hair on her arms stood up as she could feel magic wash over her. The same dread and sense of foreboding that she'd felt outside took hold of her mind. She knew it wasn't real this time, but that didn't make her run away any less.

Someone touched her shoulder and the only reason she didn't scream in fright was that at the same time, a hand was pressed against her mouth.

"It's me," Cam whispered and she calmed down. Where the waves had he been hiding? It was bright in here; not an easy place to stay hidden. She was beginning to see that the guys had been in situations like this before. The way the other two had disappeared showed they were good at this. Much better than her. She was glad she hadn't tripped over her own feet yet. That would have been very much like her. Sometimes, she forgot she didn't have four hooves.

She didn't dare whisper back in case they were noticed. But what to do now? They'd found someone, who was definitely not human, but was it a friend or foe? Why had the Staran led them here? Surely not just to see a cloaked guy do some magic tricks?

The fire circle suddenly shot up high into the air and Macey regretted her last thoughts. Maybe not just magic tricks.

Was the fire supposed to almost burn him, though? When he screamed, she realised it wasn't. Without thinking, she sent some water to him to douse the flames. To her surprise, they fought back. This wasn't normal fire. She threw her powers against it, slowly overpowering the fire with her own water magic. Steam filled the air as the flames sizzled out. With a shake of her hand, Macey poured some more water onto the circle, just to make sure.

The man was kneeling on the ground, breathing heavily. The bottom of his long black cloak had been singed and there was a smouldering hole in his hood, giving her a view of his blue hair.

Ice. They'd found Ice.

"Izban?" she asked carefully and the man jumped to his feet, his hands outstretched. Cam was in front of Macey within seconds, but she gently pushed him aside.

"We're not here to hurt you, we just want to talk."

The blue-haired man snorted. "Is that why your two companions are sneaking up on me from behind?"

Macey frowned. She couldn't see either of them. "Flint, Jared, come out! He's a friend!" Nothing happened.

He snorted again. "I'm a friend? Since when?" His hands were still outstretched and she could feel the magic in the room sizzle. There was a lot of tension waiting to explode.

"Would you care to put down your arms?" Macey asked calmly. "We're no threat to you."

"You keep saying that," he snarled. "But you attacked me!"

"I did no such thing... oh, you mean the water? But you were burning!"

"Well yes, but that's not the point! You threw water at me!"

Macey gave him a stern stare. "Would you rather have burned?"

He smiled smugly. "I don't burn."

"Because you're Ice, I know."

"What?" Now he looked more confused than angry.

Cam sighed. "What Macey is trying to say is that we know you were attacked. We know you're looking for your girlfriend and we want to help you find her.

We also know who has her and that he's setting a trap for you."

"You seem to know a lot about me, yet you haven't even introduced yourselves." Izban crossed his arms over his chest.

"Apologies, my name is Macey, and this is Camdan."

"Flint," a voice suddenly said to her right and the other two guys stepped into view.

"Where the waves have you been?" she hissed and Jared shrugged.

"Investigating." He gave Izban a little bow. "I'm Jared, at your service."

"Are you flirting with him?" Macey whispered and he shrugged again.

"I'm trying myself at diplomacy. Figured I might start practising it today."

"That was flirting, not diplomacy." She wasn't sure if she was supposed to be annoyed, jealous or amused. These men were going to be the death of her.

Izban cleared his throat. "If you know I was attacked... do you know what happened to the dog? It saved me but I couldn't stay to help her, I didn't have a chance against him."

He shuddered and Macey was tempted to do the same. Clearly, Izban had felt the Voice's touch just like her.

"She died," Macey said softly. "Her last wish was

for us to find you. Her brother brought us here, although he can't join us just now. Something is making him want to shift."

"Oh, that's me, sorry." Izban whispered something under his breath and suddenly, the flashing lights flickered out and the feeling of dread that had been assaulting Macey's heart disappeared.

"That was you? But I thought your power was ice?" Macey asked in wonder, looking at the punk with admiration. He had to be incredibly strong.

He shrugged. "It's one of my specialities. *Wicked Wards* is my online shop, you can get all the spells you need in there." He flicked his fingers and a black business card appeared in his hand. "I'm a mage," he explained when he saw their startled looks. "I'm human but I have magic. It's in the family. I inherited both my powers and the shop from my grandfather, but I've decided to take the business online. That's the future of witchcraft nowadays."

Macey continued to stare at him. He was so weird.

His expression changed as her words finally sank in. "She died? I'm so sorry. I don't know why she saved me, but I'll be forever grateful. Do you think I could speak to her brother?"

"I'm not sure. He's not very happy about her wanting us to help you. He's quite anti-human, to be honest. Better give him some time," Macey said. "If he wants to see you, he'll come."

"Fair enough. Now, why did you disturb my ritual? That's one thing you still haven't explained. Nor why you want to help me. Not many people do things out of the goodness of their hearts."

"We're like you," Macey began but Izban laughed.

"I don't think so, lady."

"Let her finish," Flint growled and a tiny flame began to flicker above Izban's head. He didn't seem to notice, though.

Macey sighed. "Have you heard about the prophecy of the Seven Wardens?"

"Yeah, Gramps made me learn all the main prophecies by heart. I found that one very strange though. Seven elements? Everybody knows there are only four."

"Me too," Macey admitted. "But I've had a bit of evidence to the contrary recently." She threw a meaningful look at Cam, who summoned a small tornado in the palm of his hands.

"Right, so you can control air," Izban said, crossing his arms and looking particularly sceptical.

"Wind, actually," Cam replied, closing his hand and extinguishing the tornado.

"Pfft, that doesn't seem likely. Especially if you think I'm part of this. I have no control over any of the four elements."

Macey sighed. She hoped Lightning and Air weren't going to be this difficult to convince. "Let's guess, you do have some ice powers though?"

"What?"

Unable to think of anything else to do, Macey flung her hand forward and let out a stream of water, sending it straight towards the blue-haired man. He threw his hands up and she watched in bemused satisfaction as the water froze mid-air and fell to the floor, smashing into thousands of tiny pieces.

"Was that really necessary?" Flint asked, chuckling to himself.

"You're one to talk," she responded, thinking of his showmanship affectionately. Flint was nothing if not a show-off. Then again, he was powerful. She imagined most people would be like that if they held his level of power.

"True."

"Did you seriously just fling fucking water at me?" Izban demanded, an indignant look on his face.

"Yes," Macey replied. "If that's the only way to get you to listen, then that's what I'm going to do. We don't have the time to mess about explaining everything to you in minute detail."

"Why not?" His nostrils flared. Macey would have laughed, but she figured that would only inflame him more. Or should that be in*ice* him? She snickered to herself. Yes, that was more like it. She could just imagine him being the cold angry type as opposed to the passionate angry one.

"Because a lot is riding on us sorting out this fucking problem." Macey just about stopped herself from stamping her foot. It was taking just about all the diplomacy skills she possessed not to do it. Something about this man just seemed to be pressing all of her buttons. Her etiquette tutor had warned her about this. She'd said that some people would wind her up regardless of what she did, and the best way to deal with them was deep breathing and counting to ten. Macey tried that. She failed.

"Who says there even is a problem?" Izban raised an eyebrow at her, while Jared shook his head behind him. Macey tried not to look at him, if she did, then she may well end up laughing, particularly as he'd now started to pull faces.

"You, for a start. You're here because your girlfriend got kidnapped, aren't you?"

"She's not my girlfriend," he muttered darkly.

"Partner? Wife? Whatever she is..."

"My sparring partner. From school." He looked at her expectantly, but all she could return was a blank stare. She had *no* idea what he was on about. "No wonder you've no idea what you're doing if you don't know such basic stuff." His eyes lit up as he threw the barb at her.

"I lived in a loch. You know, under the water. And

treat me with some respect. I'm fucking royalty," Macey blurted, letting go of any kind of restraint within her. She regretted it instantly. She shouldn't react this way.

"You know, I learned early on that anyone who has to *tell* you they're something, is usually hiding something."

"Or they've just been wound up to the extreme," she muttered darkly.

"Alright, that's enough," Cam said, stepping between the two of them and attempting to diffuse the tension that was there. Macey would've thought she'd get on with Ice instantly. If Flint was her opposite, then surely Izban should be her compliment. They should work together easily, not rile each other up.

"She started it," Izban pouted, suddenly seeming a lot younger than he had before.

"Okay," Macey sighed, before stepping around Cam. "Truce?" She offered Izban her hand, but he looked at it as if she had some kind of disease.

"Seriously, Izban, we don't have time for this," Cam said sternly. Macey admired his quiet but sure demand for respect. It was Cam all over. Flint was the showman, and Jared was a little in-your-face, but Cam was a true diplomat. He wouldn't have lost it like Macey had. She was just thankful she'd got to know the Cam beneath the mask. While she liked commanding Cam, she liked his softer side even more. Maybe because of that.

"So you keep saying."

"We can help you save Lightn–your sparring partner."

"How can you be so sure?" He was asking Cam, even though his gaze was still locked on Macey's outstretched hand. Her arm was beginning to burn with the effort, but she refused to give in. There was no way she was coming off as weak just by giving in.

"For a start, five heads are better than one," Cam said with a shrug.

"Six. Don't forget Cat-Man," Macey put in.

"Yes, but he wants to kill Izban, probably not best to give him the opportunity."

"He won't kill him. He respects his sister's wishes too much," Macey said quietly. She wasn't sure how she was so sure about that. She didn't know Cat-Man *that* well. But something within her said it was the truth. Cam nodded, acknowledging her words.

"Six heads are better than one. The second reason is that two of us can completely shield our minds. And we can teach you to do the same. It might not work all the time, but it might keep out the weaker mental threats."

"You can?" Izban's eyes widened and then moved to Macey's face, lingering there slightly.

"Yes," Cam replied. Macey's gaze flickered to him

and noted the bemused smile on his face. She wondered what that was all about, but now wasn't the time to ask more.

"Okay, fine. But only until we save Amber."

"You mean Lightning," Macey blurted, making him scowl.

"You're going to have to stop with the stupid prophecy." The hard set of Izban's eyes told her it was better just to let it drop.

"Fine." *For now,* she added in her head.

Izban finally took her hand and gave it a firm shake. About time, too. Her arm felt like it was about to drop off.

"Amber is a nice name," she said to distract him. It worked and he loosened his grip, allowing her to end the handshake.

"It is," he grumbled. "She's a nice girl. Sparring partner, I mean. One of the best. That's why I need her back."

Macey had a hard time not commenting on that. It was clear that he was head over heels in love with Lightning. But it was probably best not to tell him that; he didn't seem to like people telling him the truth. She hoped Amber was going to be more open. True, it had taken her some time to accept the prophecy, and even now she was still not a hundred percent convinced, but logically it all made sense. And logic was one thing she trusted in.

"What do we do now?" Izban asked.

"Now, you explain what kind of spell you were trying to cast," Cam said calmly, continuing to be the voice of reason. Macey wanted to hug him for being so sensible.

Izban shrugged. "A location spell to help me find her. It only lasts for about a day so I have to recast it regularly. I'm getting closer though, I thought this was the last time. But something blocked the spell and it became a little... hot."

Macey smirked, having a hard time to keep from blurting out that he'd just admitted that he'd been in trouble. So her water burst had helped him after all. Why couldn't he just admit that?

"So you think she's close?" Jared asked and Izban nodded enthusiastically.

"Yes, she can't be far, maybe a day's ride from here. I just don't know in which direction."

"Ride? Do you have a horse?" Macey asked, imagining him as the knight in shining armour riding away to save his princess. He was so un-princelike that it was hard not to laugh.

"What century do you think we live in? It's a motorbike."

"Sharara didn't mention a bike," Macey whispered to Cam, cursing herself for using the cù sìth's name a moment later. Hopefully, cat-man wasn't listening in.

"I didn't think you could take one into the Staran

either," Cam whispered back before turning back to Izban who was looking at them curiously. She hoped his hearing was as bad as that of any human. He may be a mage, but his body was human.

"How did you travel to the place where you met the dog-woman?" Cam asked, carefully phrasing his question. It was clear he didn't want to give too much away.

"A spell I tried, but it didn't work as planned," Izban explained. "It brought me to this strange foggy place, then I got attacked and fled, and suddenly I was back where I had started." He shuddered. "I never want to go there again."

"Sorry to burst your bubble, but you may have to," Macey said. It earned her a hard stare from the punk. "I don't like it much either," she added and his expression softened a tiny bit. "But it's the way we travel from A to B, so you better get used to it."

"Who says I'm going to travel with you? I've not decided yet."

Macey sighed. "Didn't we go through all of this already? We can help you find Amber. You said yourself that your location spell isn't working anymore. Maybe we can find a solution together? As much as it pains me to say this, but if the prophecy is true, we're going to need you. You're one of us, just like Amber is."

He frowned. "If we manage to get Amber away

from him, I don't want to commit to anything. It's her decision, too. If she doesn't want to stay, we can leave."

It wasn't a question. Damn that stubborn man. She was glad he was not one of her guys. Hers were much nicer. Luckily the prophecy didn't mean that she had to be with all of them. Although... how was she supposed to get his mark without... Eurgh. No, she was not going to sleep with him. He already had a girlfriend... kind of.

"That's only fair," she sighed grudgingly. Hopefully Amber was going to be nicer. She was going to have to use all her charm to get Lightning on her side. They were going to need her. It wouldn't work without all seven of them. Whatever 'it' was that they had to do to heal the Staran and stop the worlds from separating.

"Good, so what do we do now?" Izban asked, but before she could answer, a blinding pain shot through her skull.

The Voice was back.

She felt her body drop to the floor, but it was like an echo from far away amidst the pain that was racking her mind. It was so much worse than the times before. It felt as if he was closer, stronger, more brutal.

She clung to her mental barriers, begging them to stay up, but the onslaught was too much for them.

There were cracks already, quickly becoming bigger as the Voice was trying to enter her mind.

He threw pain at her and all she could do was endure.

He was almost through.

With her last conscious thought, the pictured her three men. Cam. Flint. Jared. Hopefully, they would do as she'd asked and flee. Be safe. Live a life without her. Maybe still fulfil their quest somehow. And forget her.

"I love you," she whispered as her barriers exploded into a million stars and Mahaun invaded her thoughts.

HELLO, LITTLE KELPIE. FINALLY, YOU'RE MINE.

EPILOGUE

Knowing how she was going to die was torture. Having to relive the vision each and every day, even more so. But that's what Amber had to endure ever since Mahoun had brought her here.

It was her own fault for being too cocky. There'd been a storm brewing, and she'd thought she could try and harness the power from it. She'd always had an affinity for weather magic, and this particular storm had called to her in a way she'd never experienced before. Izban had tried to tell her no. She should have listened. If she'd stayed, maybe he'd finally have acted on the feelings he so clearly had for her.

She hadn't noticed when they were still at school together; she'd been too focused on her studies to truly notice. Only after she'd been taken had she realised all the signs.

A groan came from the cell around the corner. She'd seen them when they were brought in a few days ago. Two men, probably twins, who'd been screaming something about being royalty. Not that it would help them. It didn't matter who you were down here, in the end, everybody succumbed to the darkness.

She clutched her head and screamed as pain assailed her. Even when he wasn't in the room, he was able to manipulate her mind and show her images of how she'd die. At first, she hoped the angry girl whose hair turned green, would never show up. That had been weeks ago. Now, she was praying for her to arrive and release her from her pain.

It always started the same. A new prisoner would be brought to her, a woman close to her own age. She'd be unconscious and Amber would wait for her to wake up. But that didn't happen, so Amber would go to sleep, only to wake up to being strangled by the woman. There was a lot of angry screaming, glowing eyes and hair changing colour. The girl cursing at her, green hair floating around her head in an eerie way was usually the last thing Amber saw before the vision stopped.

But every night, the green-haired woman would

follow her into her dreams. She'd taken on a life of her own. Nightmares were all Amber had nowadays.

Her days were a nightmare, her nights just the same.

She didn't even know how long she'd been here. It could easily be years.

Years of pain and dread.

She wasn't going to last much longer. She could already feel her sanity slip away.

She yawned. She wasn't going to be able to stay up much longer. She'd tried not sleeping, but it wasn't working. She'd have to face the green-haired woman again.

Maybe this time, she'd be able to kill her rather than being murdered.

Maybe.

~ FIN ~

~

Don't worry, this isn't the end of Macey's story! It continues in Into the Mists, *or get the first four books, plus bonus novellas, in the* Seven Wardens Boxed Set.

And if you want to find out more about Amber/Lightning, then read the novella Through the Storms *in which you can find out how she met Izban.*

If you enjoyed this book, we'd be really grateful if you could take a moment to write a review.

Subscribe to our newsletters for all the latest books:
Skye: skyemackinnon.com/newsletter
Laura: www.authorlauragreenwood.co.uk/p/mailing-list-sign-up.html

GLOSSARY

Adlet - Inuit descendent of a dog & human

Almas - Mongolian humanoid creature

Angakok - Inuit priest/shaman

Aos Sìth - Fairy Folk

Atliarusek - Inuit gnome sized man

Baobhan Sìth - Incubus

Beithir - Venomous Reptile, a cross between a snake and a dragon

Caladrius - a snow white bird that lives in the house of a King and can heal illness and injury

Cat Sìth - Cat Shifters

Ceasg - A mermaid with a salmon tail who can grant wishes

Cù Sìth - Dog Shifters

Daimon - Guiding Spirit (Greek)

Fàth-Fiata - Magic Fog/Mist

Fedelm - Irish Celtic Prophet

Gashadokuro - Giant Japanese skeletons that bite off heads and drink blood

Kabouter - Flemish Gnomes

Kelpie - Mythical water horse

Kludde - Flemish Shapeshifter and Trickster

Lampad - Nymphs of the Underworld who bear torches. Their light can send travelers mad

Loch - Scottish word for lake

Luch - Gaelic word for mouse

Maniilaq - Inuit 19th Century prophet

Merry Dancer - Descended from fallen angels, they now make up the northern lights

Mongolian Death Worm - underground worm

Seachd-sìona - Seven Elements

Meer - Flemish for Lake

Na Fir Gorma - Storm Kelpies/Blue Men of Minch

Seelie - Light fae folk

Selkie - Man or woman who can clothe themselves in seal skin

Sìth - Faerie/Fae

Staran - Gaelic for path

Tornak - Inuit Guardian Soul

Unseelie - Dark fae folk

Watershee - A fairy like being who often acts like a siren

ABOUT LAURA GREENWOOD

Laura is a USA Today Bestselling Author of paranormal, fantasy, and urban fantasy romance (though she can occasionally be found writing contemporary romance). When she's not writing, she drinks a lot of tea, tries to resist French macarons, and works towards a diploma in Egyptology. She lives in the UK, where most of her books are set.

Follow the Author

- Website: www.authorlauragreenwood.co.uk
- Mailing List: www.authorlauragreenwood.co.uk/p/mailing-list-sign-up.html
- Facebook Group: http://facebook.com/groups/theparanormalcouncil

facebook.com/authorlauragreenwood

twitter.com/lauramg_tdir

instagram.com/authorlauragreenwood

bookbub.com/authors/laura-greenwood

amazon.com/author/lauragreenwood

ABOUT SKYE MACKINNON

Skye MacKinnon is a USA Today & International Bestselling Author whose books are filled with strong heroines who don't have to choose.

She embraces her Scottishness with fantastical Scottish settings and a dash of mythology, no matter if she's writing about Celtic gods, cat shifters, or the streets of Edinburgh.

When she's not typing away at her favourite cafe, Skye loves dried mango, as much exotic tea as she can squeeze into her cupboards, and being covered in pet hair by her demon cat Sootie.

Subscribe to her newsletter:
skyemackinnon.com/newsletter

Join her Facebook group:
facebook.com/groups/skyesbookharem

facebook.com/skyemackinnonauthor

twitter.com/skye_mackinnon

instagram.com/skyemackinnonauthor

bookbub.com/authors/skye-mackinnon

goodreads.com/SkyeMacKinnon

amazon.com/author/skye_mackinnon

tiktok.com/@skyemackinnonauthor